The Whistle

Michael G Benningfield

The Whistle
Copyright © 2026 by Michael G Benningfield

ISBN 978-1-7368270-3-1

1

By the time winter loosens its fingers, it does not leave all at once. It lingers the way grief lingers, in small corners you forget to check. In the Ozarks, it holds on in the hollows where the sun arrives late and tired, and in the folds of the hills where snow survives like a secret. The yard behind the house had mostly gone soft again, the ground taking back its color in patches, but the shadows along the treeline still wore white. Not fresh snow, not the clean kind that makes everything look forgiven. This was the remnant stuff, gray and thinning, the last stubborn proof that cold had been here and did not want to be accused of leaving too early.

The old man noticed these things because he had trained himself to. Not for poetry. Not for pleasure. Out here, noticing kept you from slipping, kept you from breaking a hip, kept you from taking for granted a day that might decide to turn on you. He watched how the mud behaved, how the air smelled different in late February than it did in January, how the birds began to practice their voices again, tentative at first, then bolder, as if they were auditioning for a season they didn't completely trust.

That morning, the light came in thin and pale through the kitchen window, the kind of light that made coffee look like it had been poured into a jar of amber. He had been standing at the sink, hands braced on the counter, letting the warmth of the mug seep into his palms. The house was quiet except for the refrigerator's low hum and the faint ticking of the clock that he refused to replace, even though it drifted a little each month like it was trying to prove a point.

He was thinking about nothing in particular. That was what old age offered you if you were lucky: a few minutes where your mind didn't chase you like a dog. His wife was in the back room, moving gently the way she did now, careful with her knees. She had always been quiet in the mornings. Not sad-quiet. Just... reverent, like she believed the day deserved a little respect before you started making demands of it.

Then came the knock.

Not the sharp kind, not the impatient kind. Two knocks, a pause, then one more, like whoever stood outside didn't want to startle the house.

He froze with the mug halfway to his mouth.

People didn't come up the gravel drive unless they meant to. There weren't neighbors close enough for casual visits, and no one came selling anything out here unless they were lost or brave or both. His first thought was foolish and automatic: *Something's happened to the kids.* Even when your children are grown and have children of their own, your body keeps certain instincts loaded like a gun.

He set the mug down carefully. The ceramic clicked against the counter louder than it should have, like the kitchen itself was listening.

His wife called from the hallway, "You expecting someone?"

"No," he said, and his voice didn't sound like his own to him. It sounded older.

5

He moved to the front door, the boards beneath his feet giving small complaints. The air by the door was cooler, carrying the faint smell of pine and damp earth that always lived around the house in winter. He put his hand on the knob, paused, and told himself he was being ridiculous. It was probably the mail lady with a package, or a wrong turn, or some church group that had decided the backroads needed saving.

He opened the door.

A woman stood on the porch, bundled in a navy coat that looked too city-clean for the mud on the steps. She was not young, not old, somewhere in between, with hair pinned back tight and cheeks reddened by cold. She held a clipboard tucked under one arm, and in her gloved hands she carried a small cardboard box like it was fragile. Like it contained something that might break if the wind touched it too hard.

Her eyes found his and stayed there, steady but soft.

"Mr. Johnson?" she asked.

He blinked once, slow. The last name sounded strange spoken by a stranger. It always did. Names meant one thing on paper and another thing in a mouth.

"Yes," he said. "That's me."

She exhaled, the breath visible. "My name is Mrs. Caldwell. I'm with Pine Hollow Nursing Home."

The words landed without meaning at first, like a phrase spoken in another language.

Then his body understood before his mind did.

His fingers tightened on the doorframe. Not for balance. For something else.

"Pine Hollow," he repeated, and it came out rougher than he meant. "Up by—"

"Yes, sir," she said quickly, as if she had rehearsed this. "Up by the highway. I'm... I'm sorry to come without calling. We tried the number we had on file but it... it went to an old line."

He stared at her face, at the careful sorrow there, and something deep inside him began to move, slow and heavy, like a stone shifting in a river.

His wife appeared behind him. He felt her presence without turning. The house seemed to tighten around them both.

Mrs. Caldwell lifted the box slightly. "This was labeled for you. It was in his personal effects. He kept it... he kept it separate. Taped shut, with your name written on the top."

The old man swallowed, and the swallow hurt.

He looked at the box the way you look at a snake in tall grass. Not because you hate it. Because you know it can change your day.

"His?" he asked, already knowing.

Mrs. Caldwell's eyes flickered down for a moment. Respectful. "Yes, sir."

His wife's hand found his arm. Her fingers were warm through his shirt, steady as a handrail.

He heard himself say, "Come in."

Mrs. Caldwell stepped inside carefully, wiping her boots on the mat with a politeness that made his throat tighten harder. She held the box out with both hands.

He didn't take it at first.

A ridiculous thought flashed through him, bright and sharp: *If I don't touch it, it can't be true.*

But truth doesn't wait for permission. Truth sits down at your table, folds its hands, and asks you how you take your coffee.

He reached out. The box was lighter than he expected. Light enough to be cruel.

His name was written on the top in block letters, black marker pressed hard: **MR. ELIJAH JOHNSON.**

His own name, in someone else's hand, made his stomach drop.

Mrs. Caldwell spoke gently, as if she was afraid loudness might wake something in the walls. "He passed early this morning. About four-thirty. Peacefully, they said. He... he wasn't alone."

Elijah nodded, once. Twice. The motion meant nothing. His mind was already running backward down a road it hadn't traveled in years, kicking up dust, hearing the far-off whistle of a train.

His wife asked, "Was there family?"

Mrs. Caldwell's mouth tightened a fraction. "Not that we knew of. He… didn't have many visitors. But he spoke about you."

Elijah felt the room tilt, just slightly, like a boat easing away from shore.

Mrs. Caldwell added, "He couldn't always remember names. He couldn't always remember… much. But he would say there was a friend, a boy, from a long time ago. He would say you were the only one who ever—" She stopped, swallowing her own words. "I'm sorry. That's not mine to tell."

Elijah stared at the box. His hands were steady. His insides were not.

"I understand," he whispered, though he didn't. Not yet.

Mrs. Caldwell made herself smaller somehow, as if she didn't want to take up space in their grief. "There's… there's a note, too. Inside the lid."

Elijah's thumb traced the tape seam. The tape was old, yellowed at the edges. Whoever sealed it had meant it to stay sealed.

His wife stepped forward. "Elijah," she said quietly, not a question. Just his name, the way you say it when you're placing your hand on the small of someone's back as they approach a cliff.

Elijah took the box to the kitchen table and set it down like it was a sleeping child.

He pulled a chair out and sat. His knees complained. His heart didn't. His heart had gone silent, like it was waiting for instructions.

Mrs. Caldwell remained standing near the doorway. She didn't leave. She couldn't. You don't deliver something like this and then walk away like you dropped off groceries.

Elijah slid his fingernail under the tape and peeled. The sound was small but obscene in the quiet.

The lid lifted.

A folded paper rested against the inside, as promised, yellowed and creased like it had been opened and closed too many times. Beneath it sat a smaller box, darker, sturdier, wrapped in cloth.

Elijah's eyes went straight to the cloth and refused to look away.

His wife took the note carefully and opened it, her lips moving as she read. Her eyes softened, then sharpened, then filled, the way eyes do when they are trying to carry something too heavy without spilling.

She handed the paper to Elijah without reading it aloud. That was her mercy.

His hands shook for the first time.

The note was short. The handwriting was uneven, as if it had been written by a man whose body no longer did what it was told.

Eli, I kept it. I didn't use it. Not yet. Thank you for always staying and being my friend.
Love, Tommy.

Elijah read it once.

Then again, slower, like repeating it might make the years rearrange themselves.

Tommy.

He knew that Tommy didn't write the note himself. Tommy couldn't write – not with his condition. That meant someone took the time to understand what he was trying to convey and wrote the note for him. Someone, for at least a moment, cared.

The name hit him like the smell of old leather, like a radio crackling at night, like summer heat on asphalt. A name he had carried alone through marriages and funerals and jobs and children and church and moves and all the ordinary things life uses to coverup its extraordinary wounds.

His chest tightened until it felt like it might snap.

He set the note down and reached for the cloth-wrapped thing.

The cloth opened with a soft whisper, and there it was.

9

A small metal whistle, dull with age, catching the kitchen light in a way that made it seem briefly alive. A thin cord, frayed at the ends, looped through it.

Elijah's vision blurred. The room warped at the edges. He heard a sound, distant at first, like an animal caught in a fence.

Then he realized the sound was coming from him.

His body folded forward before he could stop it, and his forehead touched the table.

He did not weep politely. He wept like a child, like a man who has kept a door closed for decades and suddenly finds it blown open by a single gust.

His wife's arms came around his shoulders. She didn't hush him. She didn't tell him to be strong. She just held him, and her own tears fell onto his back like rain on dry ground.

Mrs. Caldwell stood by the doorway, eyes downcast, hand over her mouth.

From somewhere down the hall came the patter of feet.

"Grandpa?" a voice called. High and bright, still untouched by the weight of time. "Grandpa, what's wrong?"

Elijah lifted his head. His face was wet, his breathing uneven. The whistle lay on the table between his hands like a tiny, patient thing.

He looked at it, and he looked past it, through the kitchen window, through the trees, through the hills, through time.

And in his mind, he could already see the tracks again.

He could already smell Dallas dust and hear a radio announcer's voice cutting through summer air.

He could already feel the sting of fists and the sting of words.

He could already see two boys walking side by side, unwelcome on both sides of the world, and yet moving forward anyway.

He stared at his grandchild and tried to speak.

What came out was not an answer.

It was a name.

"Tommy," he whispered.

And the whistle, resting on the table, said nothing at all. It simply waited, as it always had, for the day someone would be ready to go home.

Mrs. Caldwell did not leave right away.

She stood by the door while Elijah cried, giving him the dignity of not pretending she wasn't there and the kindness of not rushing him toward composure. When his breathing finally slowed and the tears began to lose their sharpness, she stepped forward and placed the clipboard against her chest like a shield.

"I'm truly sorry for your loss, Mr. Johnson," she said. "He… he was fond of you. Even near the end."

Elijah nodded. His voice felt scraped raw, like he had swallowed gravel. "Thank you for bringing this," he said, gesturing to the box. "It matters more than you know."

She hesitated, then gave a small, careful smile. "I think he knew."

They walked her to the door. The cold rushed in when it opened, carrying the smell of wet leaves and thawing earth. The sky had brightened while they weren't looking, the gray thinning toward something that might eventually become blue.

Mrs. Caldwell stepped onto the porch, paused, then turned back. "If there's anything else we can do—"

Elijah shook his head gently. "No, ma'am. You've already done enough."

She nodded, and then she was gone, her car crunching down the gravel drive until the sound dissolved into the woods.

The house felt larger without her. Not emptier. Larger. Like grief had expanded the walls.

Elijah stood for a moment with his hand still on the doorframe, listening to the quiet settle back into its familiar places. The refrigerator resumed its hum. The clock resumed its ticking, stubborn as ever.

He exhaled.

Behind him, the children hovered.

They were his daughter's kids, all elbows and questions, still wearing the loose restlessness of a day that hadn't decided what it wanted to be yet. One of them, the youngest, peered at the table where the whistle lay, her head tilted.

"Grandpa," she said, carefully. "Who was that lady?"

Elijah closed the door and turned around.

"She was bringing me something I forgot I was still waiting on," he said.

They frowned at this, unimpressed.

The oldest, a boy with his mother's eyes and his grandfather's stubbornness, crossed his arms. "You were crying," he said. Not accusing. Just observant.

Elijah nodded. "Yes, sir. I was."

"Why?"

Elijah sat back down at the table. He didn't touch the whistle again yet. He just sat with it in his vision, the way you sit with a memory until it decides whether it's going to hurt or help.

"I lost someone," he said.

The youngest blinked. "Like... someone died?"

"Yes," Elijah said. "Like that."

There was a pause while they processed this, their faces shifting through confusion and curiosity and something quieter they didn't have a name for yet.

"But you didn't just lose him," the boy said. "You already knew he was gone. That lady said he was at a nursing home."

Elijah smiled, thin and tired. "I did know," he said. "And I didn't."

They waited. Children are good at that when they sense a story forming. They lean forward without realizing it.

"I hadn't seen Tommy in about six months," Elijah continued. "Weather wasn't kind this winter. Roads get slick up here, and I'm not as quick as I used to be. Kept telling myself I'd go once it warmed up a bit. Kept telling myself there'd be time."

His wife moved quietly around the kitchen, pouring fresh coffee, setting mugs on the table without interrupting. She knew when to fill a silence and when to let it breathe.

"I talked to him on the phone," Elijah said. "Sometimes. When he could manage it. Some days he knew who I was. Some days he didn't. Some days he'd start telling me about a baseball game from fifty years ago, like it was happening right then."

The boy's eyes widened. "That's a long time."

"It is," Elijah agreed. "But time does funny things when it starts running out."

The youngest pointed at the whistle. "Is that his?"

Elijah followed her gaze.

"Yes," he said softly. "That was his."

They looked at one another, then back at him.

"So… who is Tommy?" the boy asked.

Elijah leaned back in his chair. The wood creaked beneath him, a familiar sound. Outside, the wind stirred through the trees, just enough to make them whisper to one another.

He could have said *a friend*.

He could have said *someone I grew up with*.

He could have said *a man I knew a long time ago*.

None of it would have been true enough.

"Tommy was your uncle," he said.

Their faces lit up immediately with the relief of understanding. "We didn't know you had another brother," the girl said.

Elijah shook his head. "Not by blood."

They hesitated again, recalibrating.

"Then how?" the boy asked.

Elijah looked down at the whistle one more time, then pushed it gently back into the box and closed the lid.

"By choice," he said.

They didn't interrupt him this time.

"Some people earn their place in your life," Elijah continued. "They don't share your name or your skin or your house. But they show up when no one else does. They stay. They walk beside you when the road isn't meant for both of you."

He met their eyes, one by one.

"Tommy was family," he said. "Simple as that."

The children nodded, accepting this with the quiet seriousness children reserve for rules that feel older than adults.

Elijah stood and picked up the box. His hands were steady now.

"I think I'm going to sit outside for a bit," he said. "The air's changing."

His wife met his gaze. She didn't ask questions. She never had to.

The screen door creaked as Elijah stepped onto the porch, the sound sharp in the thinning air. He lowered himself into the old wooden chair that faced the hills, the same chair he favored when his knees ached or his thoughts needed space. The box rested on his lap, both hands folded over it like he was afraid it might drift away if he let go.

The land stretched out before him in quiet waves. Trees still bare but no longer dead-looking. Patches of snow clinging to the shaded places, stubborn as old arguments. The sky hung pale and open, undecided but leaning toward mercy.

The air carried that in-between cold, the kind that smells like damp bark and thawing earth. Spring was coming. It just wasn't finished saying goodbye to winter yet.

He sat there a moment alone.

Then the door opened behind him.

"Grandpa?" the youngest said, her voice careful, testing the space between sorrow and curiosity.

Elijah didn't turn. He smiled anyway.

"You're supposed to be inside," he said.

"We wanted to hear," the older boy said. "About Uncle Tommy."

Elijah chuckled softly at the name, a sound that surprised even him. "You already decided he's your uncle, huh?"

"You said he was," the girl replied. "Family is family."

Elijah nodded. Smart kids.

They gathered near him, one perched on the porch step, the other leaning against the railing, their breath faint and white in the air. He noticed it then, the way the cold still had teeth, the way the season wasn't ready to be trusted with young lungs yet.

"You're going to freeze yourselves," he said. "It's still a little early in the year for stories outside."

"But you promised," the boy said. "You said you'd tell us."

Elijah looked out at the hills again. The wind had gone still. Even the birds seemed to be listening.

"All right," he said finally. "I'll tell you."

Their faces brightened.

"But," he added, lifting one finger, "after I tell you, you go back inside and bundle up. Blankets, sweaters, the whole works. This cold may look like it's done, but it's got a way of sneaking back on folks who don't respect it."

They nodded solemnly, already agreeing to terms they fully intended to renegotiate later.

Elijah shifted in his chair, the wood creaking beneath him, and rested his elbows on his knees.

"Well," he said, his voice lowering, the way it always did when something mattered. "It started a long time ago. Back when I was just a boy. Back when the world was split by a set of train tracks, and neither side wanted anything to do with us."

He paused, feeling the weight of years settle into place.

"That's where I met Tommy."

The children leaned in.

And somewhere deep inside the box on his lap, the whistle waited, patient as ever.

2

The summer Dallas decided to introduce itself properly, it did so without apology.

Heat came early that year, settling over the neighborhoods like a second sky, heavier and closer than the real one. By midmorning the streets already shimmered, the asphalt breathing out a smell that mixed tar and dust and something faintly metallic. Cicadas drilled into the silence from unseen places, their noise so constant it stopped being sound and became pressure, like the city itself was thinking too loudly.

Elijah Johnson was twelve years old and already knew which sidewalks burned through thin soles faster than others.

He walked barefoot whenever he could get away with it, shoes dangling from two fingers, toes toughened by habit and necessity. His side of the tracks didn't waste leather on short distances. Besides, he liked feeling the ground. It told him things. How long the sun had been up. Whether rain had passed nearby. Whether he needed to hurry home before his mother noticed the clock moving faster than it should.

The radio voice reached him before he reached the fence.

"...and that brings Mantle to the plate, two outs, man on second—"

The sound drifted through an open window on the other side of the tracks, crackling and warbling the way AM radios did when they were working harder than they were built to. Elijah slowed. He didn't mean to. His feet just knew when to stop.

The fence itself was nothing special. Rusted wire, leaning posts, more suggestion than barrier. It ran parallel to the tracks like a tired escort, marking where one neighborhood gave way to another. The trains came through twice a day, sometimes more, roaring and clattering and shaking dust loose from everything that wasn't nailed down properly. When they passed, conversations stopped. You waited them out. That was the rule.

Elijah rested a hand on the fence and listened.

"...count now full, three and two—"

A boy sat cross-legged in the dirt about ten feet from the open window, his back to the fence, his face tipped toward the sound like it was sunlight. He rocked slightly, forward and back, forward and back, a motion so steady it looked practiced. His hair was light, almost white where the sun hit it, cut unevenly as if scissors had lost patience halfway through.

He did not look up.

"Four hundred sixty-three career home runs," the boy said suddenly.

The words burst out of him without warning, flat and exact, like a receipt read aloud. He didn't turn his head. He didn't seem to notice he'd spoken at all.

Elijah blinked.

The radio announcer droned on, oblivious.

Elijah waited, uncertain. He had learned early that some moments punished curiosity.

17

The boy rocked again.

"DiMaggio," he added, quieter. Then, louder, as if correcting himself, "Mantle has five hundred thirty-six."

Elijah leaned closer to the fence.

"You talking to me?" he asked.

No response.

The boy's fingers tapped against his knee, fast, then stopped. He rocked harder now, the dust beneath him puffing faintly with each movement.

The radio crackled. The crowd noise swelled.

"…and the pitch—"

"Curveball," the boy said. "Low. Missed."

The radio followed half a heartbeat later, confirming it.

Elijah's mouth fell open before he could stop it.

The boy stilled. For just a moment. His rocking paused, like a machine encountering resistance.

Slowly, carefully, he turned his head.

His eyes met Elijah's.

They were pale eyes. Blue, maybe gray, hard to tell in the glare. They did not flicker or dart the way Elijah expected. They fixed on him instead, intense and unblinking, like Elijah had suddenly become part of the broadcast.

The boy frowned.

"Fence," he said. "That's the fence."

Elijah straightened. "Yes, sir," he said, then immediately wondered why he'd said it like that.

The boy turned fully now, knees scraping dirt, hands pressed flat against the ground as if he needed the contact. He stared at Elijah's face, then his shirt, then his feet, then the fence again, his eyes moving in sharp, deliberate jumps.

"Train comes at two-twenty," he said. "And four-oh-five."

Elijah swallowed. "You sure know a lot about things."

The boy's head tilted. Not curiosity. Calibration.

"Tommy," he said suddenly. He tapped his chest once, hard. "Tommy Miller."

Elijah nodded. "Elijah."

Tommy's gaze slid away immediately, back toward the window, back toward the radio. The moment of connection closed as fast as it had opened.

Elijah waited. He didn't know why. Something about the boy told him rushing would break the whole thing.

The announcer's voice rose. A crack of sound, then the roar of a distant crowd.

"Home run," Tommy said. Not excited. Certain. "Right field. Second deck."

The radio lagged behind, then caught up, exploding with noise.

Elijah laughed before he meant to. A sharp bark of sound that felt almost rude in the thick heat.

Tommy flinched.

His rocking started again, faster now, his shoulders drawing in.

"Sorry," Elijah said quickly. "I just— I ain't never seen anybody do that."

Tommy's hands came up, fingers pressing against his temples like he was holding something in. His lips moved silently, counting maybe, or reciting something only he could hear.

"Four hundred thirty-seven feet," he murmured.

Elijah eased back a step, giving him space. He knew that posture. He had seen it before, back home, in his cousin Henry when the world got too loud and the numbers started tangling in his head like fishing line.

The radio finished celebrating and returned to its steady rhythm.

Tommy's rocking slowed.

He lowered his hands.

"Elijah," he repeated, softer this time. He looked at the fence again. "You're... over there."

Elijah followed his gaze. The tracks. The division. The invisible line everyone pretended was natural.

19

"Yeah," Elijah said. "I am."

Tommy nodded once, as if this confirmed something he'd already worked out.

"My daddy says you ain't supposed to be here," Tommy said.

Elijah's stomach tightened, but he kept his voice even. "My daddy says the same about you."

Tommy considered this, chewing on the inside of his cheek.

"They beat me up last week," he said abruptly. "Behind the store. Three boys. One with a stick."

Elijah felt the heat sharpen. "They do that to me, too."

Tommy looked at him again. This time, something shifted. Recognition, maybe. Or relief.

"They said I'm wrong," Tommy said. "They say words."

Elijah nodded. "They got words for everybody."

The radio voice dipped, announcing a commercial.

Tommy winced at the sudden change in volume and slapped the radio's side through the open window, adjusting it without looking.

The silence stretched.

A train horn wailed in the distance.

"Two-twenty," Tommy said.

Elijah glanced toward the tracks. "You want company?"

Tommy hesitated. His eyes flicked to the window, then to the fence, then back to Elijah.

Slowly, carefully, he scooted closer to the wire until they were separated by nothing but rust and air.

Elijah sat down on his side, mirroring him.

They listened to the game together, the sun climbing higher, the world pressing in from both directions.

Neither boy smiled.

Neither boy left.

And though neither of them knew it yet, this was the moment the world would start losing its grip on them both.

Because for the first time, neither of them was alone. The world would continue to struggle just as it does today, but in that brief moment, that small circle of time where the open window placated the world with baseball, a black kid named Elijah and a white kid named Tommy found friendship, and it would last forever.

3

At first, no one said anything.

That was the way it always started. Silence before permission, observation before judgment. The adults noticed, of course. They always did. But noticing and naming were two different things, and for a little while, the space between them was enough to let things breathe.

Elijah's mother saw it from the kitchen window.

She had been peeling potatoes into a metal bowl, the radio turned low on the counter, when she noticed him sitting by the fence again. Shoes off, knees pulled up, posture relaxed in a way that only came from feeling safe. On the other side of the wire sat the white boy, pale head tipped toward the sun, his radio balanced carefully on the dirt like it was something that could be offended if handled roughly.

They didn't speak.

They didn't have to.

The two radios played the same game, a fraction of a second apart, their voices overlapping and separating like waves. Every so often Elijah would glance up, just long enough to catch the other boy's eye. When something good happened, a hit, a steal, a clean catch, they'd grin at each other, wide and unguarded, like conspirators who had pulled off something clever without getting caught.

Elijah's mother paused, potato peeler mid-scrape.

She felt the tug of worry first. That was instinct. Then something else followed, quieter, steadier. Recognition.

She had seen that smile before. She saw it now the way she saw it years ago when Elijah was small and first learned how to make Henry laugh by tapping the table just right, by humming off-key, by understanding without asking.

She went back to peeling.

His father noticed two days later.

He came home early, shirt darkened with sweat, the lines around his eyes deeper than they had been the year before. He stopped short in the doorway when he saw Elijah through the window, his silhouette easy to spot against the fence.

He watched without speaking.

The white boy was there again. Always there. Sitting too close to where he shouldn't be. Not doing anything that could be called wrong, not exactly, but not doing anything that could be called right either.

Elijah laughed at something the radio said.

The other boy didn't laugh. He rocked. Then he smiled, slow and crooked, like the smile had to travel a longer distance to reach his face.

Elijah's father felt something old and sharp move in his chest.

He waited until supper.

They ate in the usual quiet, the clink of forks against plates, the hum of the fan trying and failing to cool the room. Elijah talked about school, about a spelling test he'd passed, about nothing in particular. He didn't mention the fence.

"Who's that boy you been sitting with?" his father asked suddenly.

The question landed heavy.

Elijah froze, fork halfway to his mouth. His mother's eyes lifted, but she said nothing.

Elijah swallowed. "His name's Tommy."

"And what's Tommy's last name?"

"Miller."

His father nodded slowly. "And where does Tommy Miller live?"

Elijah knew better than to lie. "Other side of the tracks."

His father's jaw tightened. "You don't need to be over there."

"I ain't over there," Elijah said. "He's just sittin' by the fence."

"That fence is there for a reason," his father said.

Elijah looked at his plate. The beans had gone cold.

"He don't talk much," Elijah said, choosing his words like they might crack if he squeezed too hard. "But he knows all the baseball things. Like... all of them."

His father snorted. "That don't change what he is."

His mother set her fork down. Not hard. Just enough.

"What he is," she said calmly, "is a boy."

His father shot her a look. "I'm not talking about that. You know what I mean."

"I know what you mean," she replied. "I just don't agree."

Silence thickened the room.

Elijah's father leaned back in his chair. "People see you," he said. "They see you sittin' there with a white boy, they don't see innocence. They see trouble."

Elijah's voice dropped. "People see trouble anyway."

That earned him a look sharp enough to sting.

"Eat your supper," his father said. "And stay on this side."

Elijah nodded.

He did not promise.

Tommy's father noticed it in a different way.

He noticed the dust on Tommy's pants that didn't match the yard. The way the radio was always tuned just a little lower than usual. The way Tommy's rocking slowed when he came inside, like he had already used up the energy that normally kept him balanced.

"You been wanderin' again?" his father asked one evening, beer bottle sweating in his hand.

Tommy stared at the floor.

"You talkin' to someone?" the man pressed.

Tommy's mouth opened.

"Sixteen strikeouts," he said.

His father's face darkened. "I didn't ask you about baseball."

Tommy flinched.

"He's been sittin' by the fence," the man muttered, more to himself than to Tommy. "Ain't right."

Tommy retreated to his room, the radio clutched to his chest like armor.

They found other ways to talk.

Some days Elijah brought paper and pencil. He'd draw the diamond in the dirt, bases marked with careful squares. Tommy would nod and tap the ground where the runner should go, his fingers precise, his movements certain. They played whole games without saying a word, outs and innings passing between them like secrets.

Other days they didn't bother.

They sat back to back against the fence, radios on, each listening to the same game through different static. Every so often Tommy would blurt a number. Elijah learned to recognize which ones mattered.

"Two hundred thirty-four," Tommy said once.

"Batting average," Elijah replied, and Tommy's shoulders relaxed, just a little.

When the sun dropped low and the shadows stretched long, they packed up without saying goodbye. They didn't need to. Tomorrow was assumed.

Sometimes Elijah wondered what it looked like from far away. Two boys divided by wire and history, smiling at nothing, nodding at air.

Sometimes he wondered how long the quiet would last.

Because silence, he was learning, was never empty.

It was only waiting to be filled.

4

The place was called **Henson's Market**, though everyone just called it Henson's, like adding anything more would be showing off.

It sat far enough from the tracks to pretend it belonged to no one, but close enough that both sides claimed it when convenient. A squat brick building with a faded Coca-Cola sign painted directly onto the wall, its red dulled to the color of old blood. The front windows were protected by metal bars that had long ago stopped looking temporary, and the door chimed when it opened with a tired, uneven jingle that sounded like it had given up on being cheerful.

Mrs. Miller allowed Tommy to go there alone.

That alone made it sacred ground.

She didn't say it outright, not in so many words, but Tommy understood rules when they were shaped like routines. Henson's was a straight walk. No turns. No alleys. No shortcuts. He was to leave with the radio under his arm and return with exactly what she had written on the paper. Bread. Milk. Sometimes a can of beans. Never candy unless it was payday and she was feeling generous enough to overlook the consequences.

The bell on the door calmed him. He liked that it always sounded the same, no matter who came in. He liked that Mr. Henson kept the radio behind the counter tuned to the same station every day, low enough to avoid complaints, loud enough to matter. He liked that the aisles were narrow and predictable, the shelves lined up like soldiers who knew their places.

Elijah learned about Henson's by accident.

He and Tommy had been sitting by the fence, radios murmuring in near-unison, when Tommy stood abruptly and brushed the dirt from his knees with quick, sharp swipes.

"Milk," he said. "And white bread. Store closes at six."

Elijah checked the sky. The sun had begun its slow fall, the light shifting from harsh to forgiving.

"You goin' somewhere?" Elijah asked.

Tommy nodded once. "Henson's."

Elijah hesitated. "You ain't supposed to go alone, are you?"

Tommy frowned. "I am," he said firmly. "Mom says."

There was pride in it. Fragile, but real.

Elijah weighed something in his chest. The rule his father had given him. The fence. The invisible lines that bent when no one was looking.

"I'll walk with you," he said.

Tommy stiffened. His hands fluttered once at his sides.

"Can't," he said. "Different."

"I won't go inside if you don't want me to," Elijah offered. "I'll just… walk the same direction."

Tommy considered this. His eyes moved, measuring distance, probability, risk. Finally, he nodded.

They didn't walk together so much as *alongside*. A few feet between them, enough to pretend they weren't connected if someone decided to look too closely.

Henson's smelled like floor cleaner and sugar and old wood. The bell jingled as Tommy pushed the door open, and the familiar sound settled him immediately. Elijah lingered outside, leaning against the brick wall, feeling the heat soak into his back.

Through the glass he could see Tommy moving down the aisle, careful and methodical, counting steps, whispering numbers under his breath. Mr. Henson glanced up from behind the counter, nodded once at Tommy, then glanced toward the door.

His eyes narrowed when he saw Elijah.

He said nothing.

Two white boys came in while Tommy was still inside. Older. Fourteen, maybe fifteen. All elbows and confidence, the kind that came from knowing most places already belonged to you. They glanced at Elijah, then at each other.

"Well I'll be," one of them said. "What we got here?"

Elijah straightened. "Just waitin'."

"For what?" the other boy asked, stepping closer. He smelled like cigarettes and sweat.

Elijah didn't answer.

The bell jingled again as Tommy approached the counter, milk tucked under one arm, bread under the other. He placed the coins carefully on the counter, lining them up by size.

"Two cents short," Mr. Henson said flatly.

Tommy's fingers twitched. His mouth opened.

"Fourteen cents," he said. "Milk is twelve. Bread is fourteen."

Mr. Henson sighed. "Prices went up."

Tommy froze.

Outside, Elijah watched the older boys lean closer to the window, grinning.

"Look at him," one of them snickered. "Talks to himself."

Tommy's breathing hitched. The store suddenly felt louder. The radio crackled, volume jumping for just a second.

"Elijah," Tommy said, too loud. Too sharp.

Every head turned.

29

Elijah pushed off the wall and opened the door. The bell shrieked its tired greeting.

"He's got enough," Elijah said quickly, scooping two pennies from his pocket and placing them on the counter.

Mr. Henson looked between them, then at the boys hovering near the candy rack.

"Get your stuff and go," he muttered.

Tommy clutched the bag to his chest.

The older boys blocked the door.

"Didn't know you two were friends," one said, smiling without warmth.

"We ain't," Elijah said. "We're just leavin'."

Tommy rocked. His breath came fast now, shallow.

"Sixteen strikeouts," he said. "Perfect game. Don Larsen."

The boy laughed. "What's wrong with him?"

Elijah stepped in front of Tommy without thinking.

"Move," he said.

The first punch came quick.

It caught Elijah in the shoulder, glancing but hard enough to knock him back. The second boy grabbed Tommy's arm. Tommy screamed, a raw, animal sound that tore through the store and sent the radio skidding off the counter.

"Stop!" Elijah shouted.

Mr. Henson yelled something from behind the counter, but it came too late.

A bottle shattered. Someone cursed.

And then the sound of a train horn cut through the chaos, long and furious, rattling the windows.

The boys scattered.

Tommy dropped to the floor, hands over his ears, rocking hard now, breath breaking apart.

Elijah knelt beside him, chest heaving, blood trickling from his lip.

"It's okay," he said, though it wasn't. "It's okay. I got you."

Tommy clutched his sleeve with surprising strength.

"Radio," he whispered. "Radio."

Elijah grabbed it from the floor, cracked but still alive, the game still playing as if nothing had happened.

They stayed there until the shaking stopped.

Outside, the bell jingled one last time as the door swung shut.

And the world, having shown its teeth, waited to see what they would do next.

5

The trouble didn't end at Henson's.

Trouble never did. It only changed clothes.

Elijah's mother saw his lip the moment he came through the door. Not the blood, not the swelling, but the way he held himself, careful and braced, like a boy who had already decided where the next blow might land.

"Sit," she said, and it wasn't a request.

Elijah obeyed, perching on the edge of the kitchen chair while she fetched a damp cloth. She pressed it gently against his mouth, her touch firm and practiced.

"What happened?" she asked.

Elijah hesitated.

She withdrew the cloth just enough to meet his eyes. "Try again."

"Henson's," he said. "Some boys."

Her jaw tightened. "White boys?"

Elijah nodded.

She sighed, not surprised, just tired. "And you were with him."
It wasn't a question.
"Yes, ma'am."
She replaced the cloth. "Your father's not home yet."
Elijah swallowed. "I know."

Tommy's mother didn't need to see bruises.

She heard the radio hit the table when Tommy came inside, louder than necessary, the plastic casing clattering against wood. She saw the way he bolted for the corner of the room, knees drawn up, rocking hard enough to rattle the floorboards.

"Tommy," she said softly, already crossing the room.

He covered his ears.

"Tommy," she repeated, slower, lowering herself in front of him. She waited. She always waited.

His breath came in jagged pulls.

"Hands," she said gently.

He didn't respond.

She placed her own hands in front of him, palms open, still as stone.

After a long moment, his hands slid into hers.

"Store," he said. "Boys. Loud."

She nodded. "Did someone hurt you?"

He nodded back.

"Did you fall?"

He shook his head.

"Did someone grab you?"

He nodded again, sharper this time.

She closed her eyes briefly, just long enough to be human, then opened them and pressed her forehead to his.

"You were supposed to come straight home," she whispered.

Tommy's lips trembled. "Milk," he said. "I had to."

She held him until the rocking slowed.

Elijah's father found out at supper.

He found out because Elijah's mother told him, calmly, with the same voice she used to talk about weather and bills and things that did not change no matter how loud you got.

"Some boys jumped Elijah at Henson's," she said. "He was with that Miller boy."

The fork froze halfway to Elijah's father's mouth.

"At Henson's?" he repeated. "I told him—"

"You told him not to cross the tracks," she said. "He didn't."

"That don't matter," he snapped. "People don't care about lines when they see what they want to see."

Elijah stared at his plate.

His father pushed back his chair. "I'm goin' down there."

His mother stood. "You are not."

He turned on her. "You think I'm gonna let this go?"

"I think you're gonna get yourself killed," she said evenly. "Or worse."

He laughed, sharp and humorless. "Worse than lettin' my boy get beat?"

"Worse than teachin' him fear is louder than sense," she shot back.

Elijah's heart pounded.

"I wasn't scared," he said, too quickly.

His father rounded on him. "You don't get to decide that."

Tommy's father didn't wait for supper.

He smelled the blood before he saw it, copper sharp and undeniable.

"What happened?" he barked.

Tommy flinched, rocking starting up again.

"Who did this?" the man demanded.

"Store," Tommy said. "Boys."

The bottle in the man's hand hit the wall. Glass shattered.

34

"I knew it," he snarled. "I knew you shouldn't be wanderin' around like that."

Tommy whimpered.

"And you were with him," the man continued. "That boy."

Tommy shook his head violently. "Elijah," he said. "Friend."

The word landed like a slap.

The man's face darkened. "You don't get friends," he said cruelly. "You get trouble."

Mrs. Miller stepped between them without raising her voice. "That's enough."

He turned on her. "You let him go there."

"I let him live," she replied.

The man scoffed. "That ain't livin'."

They met at the fence that night.

Not planned. Not arranged. Just the natural gravity of anger pulling things together that should never touch.

Elijah's father stood on one side, arms crossed, jaw locked. Tommy's father stood on the other, fists clenched, breath sour with drink.

"You keep your boy away from mine," Tommy's father said.

"You keep your hands off mine," Elijah's father shot back.

Tommy stood behind his mother, eyes wide, hands fluttering uselessly. Elijah stood behind his father, shoulders squared, pulse racing.

Mrs. Miller spoke first. "They're children."

Mrs. Johnson nodded. "And they didn't start this."

Tommy's father snorted. "My boy ain't right."

Mrs. Miller's voice sharpened. "He's mine."

Elijah's father glanced at Tommy, really looked this time. The rocking. The unfocused stare. The bruises blooming under pale skin.

Something flickered. Not kindness. But recognition.

"Your boy didn't throw the punch," he said slowly.

"No," Mrs. Miller said. "But he took them."

Silence stretched across the fence.

A train thundered past, shaking the ground, drowning out whatever might have come next.

When it passed, nothing had been resolved.

But something had been seen.

And sometimes, that was the most dangerous thing of all.

The fence stayed quiet after that.

Not peaceful. Just still, like the air after lightning when everyone waits to see if thunder has finished with them yet.

Elijah's father stood there longer than he meant to. He told himself he was watching the tracks, making sure no one doubled back, making sure the night didn't bring more trouble with it. But his eyes kept drifting, against his will, to the boy behind Mrs. Miller.

Tommy rocked in small, tight motions now, nothing like the frantic shaking from earlier. His hands worried the hem of his shirt, fingers twisting and untwisting as if the fabric might tell him what to do next. His eyes were fixed not on the men arguing, not on the fence, but on a loose railroad spike half-buried in the dirt near the tracks. He stared at it like it was an anchor.

Every so often, he muttered something under his breath. Numbers, Elijah's father realized. Not prayers. Not nonsense. Numbers.

The train noise faded. The cicadas crept back in, tentative at first, then bold again, filling the space the shouting had left behind.

Tommy's father broke the silence with a short, ugly laugh. "This is what happens when you let things get mixed up."

Mrs. Miller didn't answer him.

Instead, she reached back without looking and rested her hand on Tommy's shoulder. Not gripping. Just present. Tommy's rocking slowed almost immediately.

Elijah's father noticed that too.

He cleared his throat. "Your boy," he said, and stopped. The words felt unfamiliar in his mouth. "He ain't... mean."

Tommy's father scoffed. "Mean don't matter."

Elijah's father ignored him. He crouched slightly, lowering himself to Tommy's level, though he stayed on his own side of the fence.

"What's that you're sayin', son?" he asked, his voice rough but not unkind.

Tommy startled at the sound, eyes snapping up. He froze, like a deer caught halfway between flight and collapse.

Mrs. Miller inhaled sharply, ready to intervene.

"Two," Tommy said finally. "Two minutes. Until the next train. Eastbound."

Elijah's father glanced down the tracks, then back at the boy. Sure enough, a distant hum was beginning to rise, just at the edge of hearing.

"Well I'll be," he murmured.

Tommy's father rolled his eyes. "So what? He hears trains."

"No," Elijah's father said slowly. "He hears *time*."

No one spoke after that.

The train came, exactly when Tommy said it would, screaming through the night like it had somewhere important to be. The wind from it whipped dust and paper and old leaves into frantic motion. When it passed, Tommy flinched but didn't break. Mrs. Miller kept her hand steady.

Elijah's father straightened.

"You didn't start that mess at the store, did you?" he asked Tommy.

Tommy shook his head quickly. "Milk," he said. "Bread."

Elijah's father nodded. "That's what I thought."

Tommy's father snorted again, but there was less heat in it now. More confusion. The kind that unsettles a man who likes the world simple and loud.

"Come on," he muttered. "We're goin' home."

Tommy stiffened. His eyes darted to his mother.

Mrs. Miller hesitated, then nodded once. "We'll be right behind you."

Tommy's father didn't argue. He turned and stalked off, already reaching into his pocket.

Elijah's father watched him go, his jaw tightening again. Not with anger this time. With something colder.

They didn't hear the first shout clearly.

Distance muffled it, turned it into something that could almost be mistaken for frustration. Almost.

Then came the sound of something striking against wood. Or wall. Or skin. Tommy's father was throwing bottles, furniture, and anything else he could get his hands on.

Mrs. Miller had just turned to walk off, but she stopped walking as Tommy froze mid-step.

The second shout cut through the night sharper, unmistakable now. A woman's voice. Fear threaded through it like wire. Tommy's older sister. She'd catch the brunt of the drunken man on this night.

Tommy's hands flew to his ears. He dropped to the ground, rocking hard, breath tearing out of him in broken pieces.

"No no no," he whispered. "Too loud. Too loud."

Mrs. Miller knelt instantly, wrapping her arms around him, pressing his head into her chest.

"Tommy, listen to me," she murmured. "Count with me. Count."

"Six," he gasped. "Six pitches. Fastball."

"That's right," she said. "Good. Keep going."

Elijah's father stood rooted to the spot, fists clenched so tightly his knuckles burned.

Another crash echoed from the Miller house.

Elijah flinched. "Daddy—"

"Stay," his father said, without looking back.

He took one step toward the tracks, then stopped himself. He knew how this ended. He had seen it before. Men stepping into other men's houses. Men not coming back out.

Mrs. Johnson touched his arm. "You can't fix that," she said quietly. "Not tonight."

He nodded, jaw working.

The shouting inside the Miller house rose, then broke apart into something quieter but no less terrible. Crying. Pleading. The kind that doesn't ask anymore, only hopes.

Tommy rocked harder.

"Elijah," he sobbed suddenly. "Radio. Please."

Elijah didn't hesitate. He reached into his pocket and pulled out his own radio, turning the knob until the static cleared and the familiar voice poured out. Baseball. Always baseball. Safe and orderly and governed by rules that didn't change when men lost control.

Tommy latched onto the sound like a lifeline.

Mrs. Miller looked up at Elijah's parents, her eyes wet but steady. "I try," she said. "I do. But some storms don't move when you ask them."

"Rebroadcast..." Tommy said. "Already played today." He was right, it was a rebroadcast of a game played earlier in the day.

Elijah's father nodded slowly.

"He ain't broken," he said. "He's just... tuned different."

Mrs. Miller closed her eyes for a moment. When she opened them, there was gratitude there. And something like relief.

The shouting in the house died down.

The night resumed its ordinary noises.

Elijah's father exhaled, long and heavy. "My boy ain't goin' anywhere," he said. "Not from that fence. Not from your boy."

Mrs. Miller pressed her lips together, emotion threatening to spill. "Thank you," she said.

Tommy lifted his head, eyes red-rimmed.

"Elijah," he said softly. "Tomorrow?"

Elijah smiled. "Tomorrow."

The fence stood between them, rusted and thin and useless.

And for the first time, Elijah's father understood something he had never been taught how to name.

Some lines were built to keep danger out.

Others were built to keep people in.

And sometimes, the bravest thing a man could do was decide which side of the fence he stood on, even if it scared him to death.

6

Elijah had learned to ride a bicycle the hard way.

There had been no lessons, no steady hands on the seat, no warnings beyond *don't fall*. The bike had been too big for him, the road too unforgiving, and the laughter afterward had stung worse than the gravel in his knees. But he learned. Balance came the way it always did. Late. Painfully. Permanently.

That was why, when he decided Tommy should learn, he didn't ask permission.

He asked confidence instead.

The bike belonged to a boy who had moved away the previous winter, leaving it behind like an abandoned idea. It leaned against the side of Elijah's house now, paint chipped, chain squealing when you turned the pedals too fast. It was blue once. Now it was mostly memory.

Tommy stared at it like it might speak.

"Two wheels," he said. "That's unstable."

Elijah grinned. "Everything starts that way."

They stood near the dirt road that curved away from the fence, far enough from the tracks to avoid the trains, close enough to run if they had to. The ground there was packed firm from years of passing feet and tires. Safer than asphalt. Safer than concrete. Elijah had thought it through. Mostly.

"You just gotta trust it," Elijah said, holding the handlebars steady. "You don't think about each wheel separate. You think about goin' forward."

Tommy's fingers hovered inches from the grips. His hands trembled.

"Forward is… variable," he said.

Elijah softened his voice. "I ain't gonna let go."

That mattered.

Tommy nodded once and climbed onto the seat, movements stiff and careful, like he was assembling himself in the wrong order. His feet searched for the pedals, missed, found them again.

"Elijah," he said. "If I fall—"

"You might," Elijah said honestly. "But you also might not."

Tommy absorbed this, eyes flicking to the road, to the fence, to the sky.

"Okay," he said.

Elijah started walking, one hand on the seat, one on the handlebars, matching Tommy's uneven pedal strokes. The bike wobbled immediately.

"No no no," Tommy muttered. "Wrong. Wrong."

"You're doin' fine," Elijah said. "Just keep lookin' ahead."

Tommy looked down.

The front wheel jerked.

Elijah tightened his grip. "Eyes up!"

Tommy obeyed, snapping his gaze forward, and for half a second, everything aligned. The bike straightened. The pedals turned. The road smoothed out beneath them like it had been waiting.

Tommy's mouth opened in surprise.

"I'm—" he began.

Elijah let go.

Not on purpose. Not completely.

Just enough.

The bike surged forward, suddenly unanchored, suddenly alive. Tommy yelped, a sharp sound torn free from somewhere deep. His legs froze. The pedals spun uselessly beneath his feet.

"Elijah!" he cried.

The bike veered.

The front tire hit a rut.

Tommy went down hard.

The sound was wrong. Too solid. Too final.

Elijah ran.

Tommy lay twisted in the dirt, breath knocked clean out of him, eyes wide and unfocused. Blood seeped from a scrape along his arm, bright and immediate.

"Tommy," Elijah said, dropping to his knees. "Tommy, look at me."

Tommy gasped, then screamed.

Not from pain. From overload.

His hands flew to his head. His body curled inward, rocking violently now, heels digging trenches in the dirt.

"No no no," he sobbed. "Too fast. Too loud. Too wrong."

Elijah panicked.

He grabbed Tommy's shoulders, then pulled his hands back, remembering too late what helped and what didn't.

"I'm sorry," he said, voice breaking. "I shouldn't have— I thought—"

Tommy's scream cut him off.

Footsteps pounded toward them.

Elijah looked up, heart slamming, expecting fathers, fists, consequences.

Instead, a man stood at the edge of the road.

He hadn't been there a moment before.

He was tall, thin, dressed in a coat too heavy for the day, the fabric worn soft with age. His hair was dark but threaded with gray, his face lined in a way that suggested weather rather than years. His eyes were calm. Too calm.

He took in the scene in one sweep. The fallen bike. The bleeding arm. The boy unraveling in the dirt. The other boy kneeling helplessly beside him.

"Easy," the man said.

The word did not ask. It *settled*.

Tommy's screaming faltered, just a fraction.

The man crouched at a careful distance, not touching, not intruding.

"You're still here," he said, his voice steady and low. "You didn't go anywhere."

Tommy's breath hitched.

The man nodded. "That's right. You stayed."

Elijah stared. "Sir—"

The man lifted a finger gently. "Let him finish first."

Tommy's rocking slowed. His breaths stretched longer, less jagged.

The man waited.

When Tommy finally looked up, eyes glassy and red, the man smiled faintly.

"You're good with numbers," he said.

Tommy nodded automatically.

"And you like baseball."

"Yes."

The man reached into his coat pocket.

"This is for you," he said, holding out a small object on an open palm.

A whistle.

Simple. Metal. Dull in the sunlight.

Tommy stared at it.

"What's that?" Elijah asked.

The man looked at him then. Really looked.

"A kindness," he said. "And a warning."

Tommy reached for it, then froze, fingers trembling.

"Only one use," the man continued calmly. "You don't blow it unless you're ready to go home. All the way home."

Elijah's stomach dropped. "Home like... your house?"

The man smiled, not unkindly. "No."

Tommy's fingers closed around the whistle.

"What happens if I blow it?" he whispered.

The man's eyes softened. "God comes and gets you," he said. "Because you've had enough."

Elijah laughed nervously. "That ain't funny."

The man stood. "I didn't say it was."

He stepped back, already fading into the edges of the day.

"Be mindful of where you stand," he said. "And who you help up."

Then he was gone.

Not walking away.

Just... gone.

Elijah looked around wildly. "Did you see where he went?"

Tommy shook his head, clutching the whistle to his chest.

"Too quiet," he said.

Elijah helped him sit up, heart racing, questions piling up faster than answers.

"You okay?" Elijah asked.

Tommy nodded slowly. "I fell," he said. "But I didn't go."

Elijah swallowed.

They sat there together, the bike forgotten, the road empty, the whistle cold and heavy between them.

Neither boy laughed it off.

Neither boy tried it.

And somewhere far away, a train blew its horn.

Right on time.

They didn't pick the bike up.

Elijah thought about it, just for a second. The chain lay slack in the dirt, one pedal bent inward like a broken wing. But when Tommy tried to stand, his knees wobbled and his hands went straight back to the whistle, fingers wrapping around it with a grip that said *this stays with me*.

"Leave it," Elijah said quietly. "I'll get it later."

Tommy nodded, already turning his back on it like the decision had been made somewhere deeper than words.

They walked home by a longer route, cutting through the trees where the ground dipped and rose unevenly. Elijah stayed half a step ahead, watching corners, listening for voices that didn't belong to the woods. The air had cooled, the heat breaking just enough to make the breeze feel earned.

Tommy moved stiffly, but he moved.

Every few steps, his hand lifted to his chest, checking.

Still there.

"You okay?" Elijah asked for the third time.

Tommy nodded. "Scrapes heal," he said. "Time constant."

Elijah smiled faintly. "You sure say things funny."

Tommy considered this. "You talk too much."

Elijah laughed, then caught himself, glancing around.

They reached the edge of the clearing near the road and froze.

Voices drifted in from ahead. Two boys. Maybe three. Laughter sharp and careless.

Elijah cursed under his breath.

"Bullies?" Tommy whispered.

"Maybe," Elijah said. "Probably."

Tommy's breathing quickened.

"Hey," Elijah said softly. "Look at me."

Tommy did. Immediately. That part had gotten easier.

"We ain't gonna be here," Elijah said. "Not long enough for them to notice."

He pointed toward the ditch line, where weeds grew tall and thick. "We go low. Quiet."

46

Tommy nodded, crouching without being told.

They moved through the weeds like something practiced, Tommy surprisingly careful now, placing his feet where Elijah did, matching his pace. The whistle bumped softly against his chest with each step.

One of the boys laughed again, closer now.

"Elijah," Tommy whispered. "Heart's fast."

"I know," Elijah whispered back. "Mine too."

They waited, still as stones, until the laughter faded.

When it was safe, they continued.

Only when the fence came into view did Elijah let his shoulders drop.

They stopped there, breathless.

Tommy leaned against the wire, chest heaving, then laughed. A strange sound. Sharp and sudden and too loud.

Elijah stared at him. "What's funny?"

Tommy shook his head. "Man appeared," he said. "Then didn't."

Elijah felt a chill crawl up his spine. "You think he was real?"

Tommy frowned. "He talked. He gave me an object. Objects are real."

Elijah thought about that. "People talk in dreams, too."

Tommy's eyes flicked down to the whistle. He rubbed his thumb over the metal, slow and deliberate.

"Dreams don't leave weight," he said.

Elijah swallowed.

They sat there, backs to the fence, dusk settling around them like a held breath.

"What if he's wrong?" Elijah asked. "What if it's just a whistle?"

Tommy tilted his head. "Then nothing happens."

"And what if he's right?"

Tommy didn't answer immediately.

Finally, he said, "Then I don't use it."

Elijah nodded. "Good plan."

Tommy looked at him. "You can't."

Elijah blinked. "Can't what?"

"Use it," Tommy said. "It's not for you."

Elijah frowned. "Why not?"

Tommy's gaze was steady. "Because you're not done."

The words hit harder than Elijah expected.

They sat until the sun slipped low enough to stain the sky orange and purple, until the cicadas took over from the birds, until the world felt normal again, or at least familiar.

When they finally stood, Tommy tucked the whistle beneath his shirt, out of sight.

"Tomorrow?" he asked.

Elijah nodded. "Tomorrow."

They separated at the fence, each turning toward a home that felt a little less solid than it had that morning.

Behind them, the abandoned bike lay where it had fallen, slowly cooling in the dirt.

And the whistle, warm against Tommy's chest, waited.

7

The wind had shifted by the time Elijah finished.

Not much. Just enough to carry the smell of thawing leaves and wet stone up onto the porch. The children sat close now, knees tucked under chins, jackets pulled tight the way Elijah had told them to. They had listened without interrupting, eyes wide, hands forgotten in their laps.

For a long moment, no one spoke.

Then the oldest cleared his throat.

"Why were they so mean to you?" he asked. Not angry. Just confused. "You didn't do anything."

Elijah smiled faintly. He'd asked himself that same question more times than he could count.

"Sometimes people are taught fear before they're taught kindness," he said. "And once fear settles in, it starts looking for somewhere to land."

The boy frowned. "That's dumb."

Elijah chuckled. "It is. But dumb things tend to stick around."

The youngest shifted closer. "What was wrong with Uncle Tommy?" she asked, careful with the words, like she was stepping on thin ice. "Why did he talk funny and shake like that?"

Elijah looked down at his hands. They were older now. Lined. Steadier than they had any right to be.

"Nothing was wrong with him," he said gently. "Not the way folks meant it back then."

She tilted her head. "Then why was he different?"

Elijah thought for a moment, searching for something small enough to fit into a child's understanding without losing its shape.

"Some people's brains are like radios," he said. "Most folks have theirs tuned the same way. Same stations. Same volume. Tommy's was tuned differently. He picked up things other people couldn't. Numbers. Patterns. Sounds."

"And the shaking?" the boy asked.

"That was his body trying to keep up," Elijah said. "When the world got too loud or too fast, it was how he held himself together."

The girl considered this. "Did it hurt him?"

"Sometimes," Elijah admitted. "Mostly when people didn't bother trying to understand."

The boy's brow furrowed. "Did you understand him?"

Elijah smiled. "I tried."

The youngest leaned forward. "Is that why he was your best friend?"

Elijah nodded. "That's exactly why."

They sat with that for a moment, the hills stretching quietly and patient before them.

"Did the whistle really call God?" the girl asked suddenly.

Elijah laughed softly. "That's a big question."

"Is it real?" she pressed.

"The whistle? Yes, it's very real. That's what is in this box on my lap. The whistle. The reminder of everything that kept us together and almost tore us apart at the same time."

Elijah looked out toward the trees, toward the places where winter still clung in thin white ribbons. "Now, does it really call God and send you off to Heaven? I don't know," he said honestly. "I just know we never used it. Not when we were boys."

The boy squinted. "Why not?"

Elijah's voice lowered. "Because we weren't ready to go home yet."

They were quiet again, but this time it felt settled, not heavy.

Elijah leaned back in his chair, the wood creaking beneath him. "You still want to hear the rest?"

They nodded eagerly, three heads bobbing in unison.

"Okay," he said. "But this part's important."

He closed his eyes, just for a second, and let the porch dissolve.

Then

The next morning dawned thick with heat and dust, the kind that made everything feel closer than it should. The fence waited, rusted and familiar, and two radios crackled to life like nothing strange had ever happened.

Tommy arrived late.

He walked stiffly, favoring one side, his shirt buttoned crooked. The whistle was hidden beneath it, the cord looped tight around his neck.

Elijah saw it immediately.

"Hey," he said. "You all right?"

Tommy nodded once. "I dreamed," he said.

Elijah's stomach dipped. "About the man?"

Tommy shook his head. "About falling. And not."

He sat carefully, hands pressed flat to the dirt, grounding himself.

"Elijah," he said softly. "If the man was real…"

Elijah leaned closer. "Yeah?"

"Then he knew us," Tommy finished. "Before."

Elijah had no answer for that.

The radio announcer's voice rose, steady and reassuring.

51

And the world, pretending to be ordinary again, waited for the boys to keep growing up.

8

The whistle changed nothing.

That was the lie Elijah told himself at first.

Life went on the way it always had. The fence stayed where it was. The tracks kept dividing the town cleanly enough for people who liked their lines straight. Radios still crackled with baseball games, and boys still learned the limits of their bodies the hard way. If you looked from far enough away, nothing had shifted at all.

Up close, everything had.

Tommy touched the whistle more than he talked about it. His fingers found it when voices rose, when footsteps came too fast from behind, when the air itself felt sharp. He never lifted it to his lips. Never tested it. But it lived against his chest now, warm and solid, like a thought he couldn't put down.

Elijah noticed.

The first time was small. A group of boys gathered near the fence one afternoon, not saying much, just watching. Staring. The kind of silence that pretends to be harmless until it isn't. Tommy's rocking picked up, shallow and quick, his breath tightening.

Elijah nudged him. "Hey. Game's on."

Tommy nodded, but his hand slipped beneath his shirt.

"Elijah," he whispered. "If it gets bad…"

Elijah's heart thumped. "It won't."

"But if it does."

Elijah followed Tommy's gaze to the far end of the street, where shadows stretched long and uncertain. "You don't use it," he said firmly. "Not for them."

Tommy's fingers tightened around the metal.

"Only one use," he murmured.

"Exactly," Elijah said. "That's why you don't waste it."

Tommy let out a shaky breath and loosened his grip.

The boys drifted away eventually, bored or distracted or pulled elsewhere by something louder. The danger passed, but the feeling didn't. Elijah understood then that the whistle wasn't just a thing. It was a question that never stopped asking itself.

School made everything worse.

It started with whispers. Notices sent home folded too neatly. Teachers speaking carefully, like they were stepping around broken glass. Words like *integration* and *adjustment* floated through the halls without ever quite landing.

Then came the first day.

Elijah walked into class with his shoulders squared, his face neutral, every lesson his parents had ever taught him pressed tight against his spine. He counted desks. Counted exits. Counted eyes.

Some kids stared openly. Others refused to look at him at all. A few smiled too hard, the way people do when they're trying to convince themselves they're being kind.

Tommy sat two rows over, rocking slightly, his gaze fixed on the chalkboard even before the teacher arrived. The whistle cord was tucked beneath his collar, invisible but present. Elijah could tell when Tommy's hand brushed it. The movement was subtle now. Practiced.

The teacher cleared her throat. "Let's all remember," she said, voice strained, "that we are here to learn."

Someone snorted.

Someone else muttered a word Elijah pretended not to hear.

Tommy flinched.

"Tommy," Elijah whispered, barely moving his lips.

Tommy's eyes flicked toward him, wide and searching.

"You're okay," Elijah said. "Just breathe."

Tommy nodded, rocking slowing by degrees.

The day dragged. Pencils scratched too loudly. Chairs scraped too sharply. Every sound felt amplified, like the building itself was listening.

At recess, the line between sides didn't vanish. It just moved.

Kids clustered by habit. By skin. By fear. Elijah stood alone near the fence that bordered the playground, hands in his pockets, watching Tommy pace in tight circles nearby.

Three boys approached.

"You don't belong here," one of them said.

Elijah met his gaze. "Teacher says I do."

The boy sneered. "Teacher don't know nothin'."

Tommy stopped pacing. His breath hitched.

"Elijah," he said, too loud.

The boy turned. "What's wrong with him?"

Tommy's hand flew to his chest.

The whistle pressed into his palm, solid and sure.

Elijah saw it then, clear as day. The temptation. The simple math of it. One breath. One sound. Everything stops.

He stepped forward fast.

"Hey," he said sharply, snapping Tommy's focus back to him. "Look at me."

Tommy's eyes locked on.

"You hear the game last night?" Elijah asked.

55

Tommy blinked. Confused. Distracted.

"Three home runs," Elijah continued. "All in the fifth."

Tommy swallowed. "Mays," he whispered. "Two of them."

"That's right," Elijah said. "You tell me about it."

The boys scoffed and walked away, disappointed by the lack of spectacle.

Tommy sagged like a string cut loose.

"That was close," he said.

Elijah nodded. "Too close."

Tommy looked down at the whistle in his hand. "It would have stopped."

Elijah's voice dropped. "It would've ended."

Tommy considered that.

Slowly, he tucked the whistle back beneath his shirt.

Dallas simmered that year.

Protests downtown. Police lines. Shouted words that echoed off brick buildings and lodged themselves in young minds like splinters. Adults argued in kitchens and living rooms, their voices carrying through walls children pretended not to hear.

At night, Elijah lay awake listening to the radio not for baseball, but for news. For the sound of the world changing whether anyone liked it or not.

Some nights, he imagined the whistle between his own fingers. Cold. Certain.

He never touched it.

Because even when things were bad, even when the ground felt like it was shifting beneath them, there was still Tommy sitting by the fence. Still radios playing the same game. Still tomorrow waiting, stubborn and unfinished.

The whistle waited too.

Not as a promise.

As a reminder.

And the boys, growing older and more aware by the day, learned something most people didn't realize until it was too late.

That sometimes the bravest thing you can do is stay.

Especially when leaving would be easier.

9

By the time summer leaned fully into itself, Dallas no longer pretended to be polite.

The heat pressed down harder, like it had chosen a side. Streets filled faster. Sirens became background noise. Adults spoke in clipped sentences that stopped whenever children entered the room, as if truth were something sharp enough to cut young skin.

Elijah felt it everywhere.

At school, desks were rearranged again and again, like the teachers believed order itself might convince everyone to behave. Names were called slower during attendance, every unfamiliar one weighed carefully in the mouth. Some kids stopped coming altogether. Others showed up flanked by parents who stood stiffly at the back of the room, daring the day to go wrong.

Tommy showed up every day.

That alone felt like defiance in a world where chaos was beginning to be the norm.

He sat in the same seat, hands folded tight when the room grew loud, rocking just enough to keep himself anchored. The whistle stayed hidden beneath his shirt, the cord tucked flat against his skin. Elijah knew exactly when Tommy touched it. The movement was small, almost nothing. But Elijah watched for it the way sailors watch the horizon.

One morning, the principal stood at the front of the room with a man Elijah didn't recognize. The man wore a suit too heavy for the heat and smiled like he expected trouble but hoped it might wait until lunch.

"Starting next week," the principal said, "there will be some changes."

Nobody asked what kind.

They all already knew.

The fence didn't feel as safe as it once did, when we first met on that crisp day.

Kids lingered near it now, not to listen to baseball, but to watch. To count who crossed where. To see who dared. The radios still played, but they competed with raised voices and laughter that wasn't meant to be shared.

One afternoon, Elijah found Tommy already there, pacing instead of sitting.

"Too many," Tommy said. "Too many variables."

Elijah followed his gaze. Four boys down the street. Older. Watching.

"They ain't doin' nothin'," Elijah said, though he didn't believe it.

"Yet," Tommy replied.

The whistle pressed visibly against his shirt.

Elijah stepped closer. "Hey. Eyes on me."

Tommy obeyed instantly.

"You remember what we said," Elijah continued. "That whistle ain't for fear."

Tommy swallowed. "Fear is loud."

"Yeah," Elijah said. "But it passes."

Tommy hesitated. "Pain doesn't."

Elijah didn't have an answer for that.

The boys down the street shouted something unintelligible and laughed. One of them mimed blowing a whistle, puckering his lips exaggeratedly.

Tommy flinched.

Elijah felt something cold settle in his stomach. Not fear. Decision.

"Come on," he said. "We're leavin'."

Tommy resisted for half a second, then followed.

They didn't go toward home; they didn't go toward the safety net that had always been there to keep others out. This day, they did something different.

They went toward the tracks.

The train yard was off-limits. Everyone knew that. Not because there were signs, but because adults spoke about it in the same tone they used for graveyards and deep water.

Elijah had been there once before, years ago, chasing a ball that rolled too far. He remembered the smell. Oil and rust and heat. A place where nothing forgave mistakes.

Tommy stopped at the edge of it, breathing fast.

"Not safe," he said.

"Neither is stayin'," Elijah replied. Instinctively he reached out for Tommy's hand, to let him know it was OK. Tommy shrank back and kept his hand to himself, and Elijah remembered — touch is as dangerous as sound. He motioned for Tommy to follow him forward.

They crouched behind a line of stacked railroad ties, splintered and sun-bleached. The ground vibrated faintly beneath them, a distant engine humming like something asleep but dreaming.

Tommy pressed his palms flat against the dirt.

"Elijah," he whispered. "If a train comes—"

"We'll hear it," Elijah said. "You always do."

Tommy nodded, reassured by the logic.

They sat there longer than Elijah intended. Long enough for the shouting back near the fence to fade. Long enough for the sun to slide just enough to take the worst edge off the heat.

Tommy's rocking slowed.

"Elijah," he said quietly. "Why do they hate?"

Elijah stared out at the rails stretching away, shining and merciless.

"Because someone taught them," he said. "And no one bothered to un-tell it."

Tommy considered this.

"My daddy hates," he said flatly.

Elijah's jaw tightened. "Yeah. I know."

Tommy looked at him. "Does your daddy?"

Elijah hesitated. "He's… learnin'."

Tommy nodded, satisfied with that.

A train horn blew suddenly, closer than Elijah expected.

Tommy stiffened. His hand flew to his chest.

"Wait," Elijah said quickly. "It's still far."

Tommy listened, head tilted, counting silently.

"Three minutes," he said. "Plenty."

His hand fell away from the whistle.

Elijah let out a breath he hadn't realized he was holding.

They stayed until it felt safe to return.

That night, Elijah lay awake listening to the radio, turned low beside his bed. The announcer's voice drifted in and out, steady and comforting. He thought about the whistle. About how close it had come to being used for something small. Something temporary.

He thought about how easy it would be to want out when the world pressed too hard.

In the dark, he made himself a promise. He would be the one who stayed calm. He would be the one who spoke first.

61

He would be the one who reminded Tommy that there was still a tomorrow worth waiting for.

Outside, a distant train passed through the night.

And somewhere between its beginning and its end, two boys learned that growing up wasn't about getting stronger.

It was about learning when not to give up, and soon, they'd learn what trust really meant when all the odds are stacked against you.

10

Trust was easy when no one was looking.

It lived comfortably by the fence, in the quiet math of radios and glances and shared shade. It thrived in places where trouble could be heard coming and avoided if you were quick enough. But trust, Elijah was learning, behaved differently when it was dragged into the open and asked to perform.

The test came on a Saturday.

The town had decided it needed a parade.

No one said it out loud, but everyone understood why. A show of order. Of unity. Flags, marching bands, uniforms pressed sharp enough to cut through doubt. The kind of event adults planned when they wanted to remind themselves that they were still in charge of how things looked.

Elijah's father didn't want him anywhere near it.

"Too many people," he said. "Too many tempers."

Elijah's mother hesitated longer than usual before agreeing. "Stay close," she told him. "Don't run your mouth. And come straight home."

Elijah promised.

He didn't promise Tommy wouldn't be there.

They found each other near the edge of the crowd, where the street widened and the noise hadn't yet piled up on itself. Brass instruments flashed in the sun. Drums rattled ribs. People pressed shoulder to shoulder, heat and excitement turning bodies careless.

Tommy stood stiffly beside Elijah, hands clenched at his sides, jaw working like he was chewing on something invisible.

"Too loud," he said. "Too many."

Elijah nodded. "I know."

Tommy's hand twitched toward his chest and stopped. He looked at Elijah instead.

"Stay," he said.

"I'm not goin' anywhere," Elijah replied.

They watched the band pass, then the fire trucks, then the men in suits waving like the world hadn't been arguing with itself for months. A few people noticed them. A few frowned. Most pretended not to.

Then someone shoved.

Not hard. Just enough.

Tommy stumbled.

The noise surged around them, laughter and shouting colliding until Tommy's breath shortened, his rocking starting in sharp, panicked bursts.

"Elijah," he said. "Can't—"

"I got you," Elijah said immediately.

A boy nearby snorted. "What's wrong with him?"

Another voice chimed in. "Looks broke."

Tommy's breathing went ragged.

The whistle pressed hot against his chest now, undeniable.

Elijah stepped in front of him without thinking, back straight, feet planted.

"Don't," he said.

The boys laughed. "Or what?"

Elijah felt the eyes then. Adults. Kids. Curious and hostile and bored all at once. The parade kept moving. No one stopped.

Tommy made a sound low in his throat. His fingers curled tight around the whistle cord.

"Elijah," he whispered. "I need—"

"No," Elijah said softly but firmly. "You need me."

He turned just enough so Tommy could see his face.

"Look at me," he said. "Count with me."

Tommy's eyes locked on.

"Bases," Elijah said. "Tell me."

"Four," Tommy breathed. "Square. Ninety feet apart."

"Good," Elijah said. "Now innings."

"Nine," Tommy said. "Sometimes more."

The crowd noise dimmed for Tommy, pulled back by focus and familiarity. His rocking slowed. His grip loosened.

One of the boys scoffed and shoved Elijah's shoulder.

Elijah didn't move.

"You ain't scared?" the boy asked.

Elijah swallowed. His heart was hammering so hard he could feel it in his teeth.

"Yes," he thought.

"No," he said.

A hand landed on the boy's arm. A grown man. Stern voice. "That's enough."

The boys backed off, disappointed.

Elijah didn't turn around until Tommy's breathing evened out completely.

"It passed," Tommy said, wonder in his voice.

Elijah nodded. "Told you."

They stood there a moment longer, then slipped away while the parade distracted itself.

They walked home in silence.

At the fence, Tommy stopped.

"You didn't leave," he said.

Elijah shrugged. "I said I wouldn't."

Tommy looked down at the whistle, then back up. "I trusted you."

Elijah felt something settle in his chest. Heavy. Permanent.

"Yeah," he said. "Me too."

Behind them, the parade kept marching, loud and proud and certain of itself.

And two boys, unseen now, had learned that trust wasn't about safety.

It was about staying, even in the toughest of times, and times were about to get tougher.

Elijah watched Tommy walk through the rundown yard, open the broken wooden gate, and close it behind him, shoulders still a little tight but steady. Only then did Elijah head the other way, dust clinging to his shoes, the echo of drums and brass still rattling around in his ears.

Home felt quieter than it should have.

His father sat in the front room with the radio on low, pretending to read the paper. His mother moved through the kitchen without humming, which Elijah noticed right away. The parade noise had drifted past the house earlier, cheers and music bouncing off brick and glass, but now there was only the hum of electricity and the distant sound of voices settling back into their normal places.

"You alright?" his mother asked.

"Yes, ma'am," Elijah said. It was mostly true.

Later, when the sun dipped enough to take the edge off the heat, Elijah slipped back outside. Tommy was already there, sitting on his side of the fence with his radio balanced on his knees, antenna angled just so. Elijah sat opposite him, close enough that the static overlapped, close enough to feel anchored again.

Preseason baseball didn't matter the way the real games did, but they listened anyway. The voices were familiar. Predictable. Safe.

Tommy rocked gently, relaxed now, eyes half-lidded.

"Lineup's wrong," he murmured. "They'll fix it."

Elijah smiled. "You always say that."

"They always do," Tommy replied.

The announcer's voice droned on, describing a routine fly ball, the crack of bat against ball snapping through the air like punctuation.

Then the voice changed.

It wasn't loud. It didn't need to be.

There was a pause, a breath taken somewhere far away, and when the announcer spoke again, the rhythm was gone.

"We interrupt this broadcast," the man said, his words careful and heavy, "to bring you some breaking news."

Tommy stilled.

Elijah felt it before he understood it, a tightening in his chest that had nothing to do with fear and everything to do with recognition. Adults only spoke like that when the world had shifted.

The announcer continued. "Dr. Martin Luther King Jr. was shot earlier this evening in Memphis, Tennessee. We are now receiving confirmation that he has died."

The words hung there, unfinished, like the sentence itself didn't want to exist.

Elijah's mouth went dry.

Tommy blinked. Once. Twice.

"Died," he repeated quietly. "Permanent."

The radio crackled as the announcer struggled to continue, voice strained, the studio suddenly too small to hold what had just happened.

For a moment, there was no sound at all from the neighborhood.

Then it came.

A cry, sharp and raw, from somewhere down the street. Another voice answered it, angry, loud, breaking apart. Doors slammed. Someone shouted a name. Someone else shouted a word Elijah had heard before but never this close together, never this loud.

Tommy's rocking started again, faster now.

"Elijah," he said, breath hitching. "Something's wrong."

Elijah didn't answer. He couldn't. His eyes had gone to the street beyond the fence.

Henson's was in view from where they sat, the same squat brick building that had watched them bleed and leave and come back stronger. The parade route ran right past it. People were still there, clustered and confused, some crying openly now, others shouting, fists raised, words spilling out like fuel.

A bottle shattered against the curb.

Someone screamed.

The sound rolled toward them, swelling, folding in on itself. Sirens began to wail in the distance, their pitch rising and falling like something wounded.

Tommy pressed his hands to his ears.

"Too much," he whispered. "Too fast."

Elijah moved closer to the fence, lowering his voice. "Hey. Look at me."

Tommy's eyes flicked up, a wildness in them that was never there before.

"They killed him," Elijah said, not knowing who *they* were yet, only knowing the weight of it. "They killed a man who was tryin' to make things better."

Tommy's breathing went shallow. His hand slid beneath his shirt. The whistle.

"Elijah," he said. "If people start hurting—"

"No," Elijah said immediately. "Not like this."

"But it would stop," Tommy insisted, his fingers curling around the metal. "Everything stops."

Elijah's heart pounded. He could hear shouting now, close enough to catch words, to recognize anger when it shed its skin.

"It wouldn't fix it," Elijah said, leaning forward until his forehead touched the fence wire. "It wouldn't bring him back."

Tommy hesitated.

The radio shifted again, cutting to more voices, more disbelief, more grief poured through wires not built to carry it.

A group of men rushed past Henson's, one of them knocking over a trash can, another kicking it hard enough to send it skidding into the street. Someone threw a rock. Glass burst outward in a glittering wave.

Tommy flinched violently.

"Elijah," he cried.

Elijah didn't think. He climbed the fence.

Not all the way. Just enough to lean across, to reach through the wire and grab Tommy's wrists.

"Stay," he said fiercely. "Stay with me."

Tommy's grip on the whistle tightened, then loosened.

"I don't want to go," he sobbed. "I just want it quiet."

"I know," Elijah said, voice breaking. "Me too."

They stayed like that, hands tangled through rusted wire, the world unraveling within sight and sound of them. The whistle remained unblown. The fence held. Barely.

Eventually, adults shouted names. Lights flicked on. Someone yelled at everyone to get inside.

Tommy's mother appeared at the edge of the yard, face pale, fear written plain across it.

"Tommy!" she called.

Tommy pulled back, chest heaving.

"Tomorrow?" he asked Elijah, desperate.

Elijah nodded. "Tomorrow."

Tommy ran.

Elijah climbed down and stood alone as night fell hard and fast, sirens cutting through the dark, the radio still murmuring words that would change the country forever.

The parade was gone now, trampled into something unrecognizable.

And Elijah understood, standing there in the gathering chaos, that trust was no longer just about each other.

It was about believing the world could survive what it kept doing to itself.

And that belief, he knew, was going to be tested next.

11

Monday came anyway.

It arrived dressed like any other school day, buses hissing to a stop, doors slamming, teachers forcing smiles that didn't quite fit their faces. But something underneath it all had shifted. The air felt brittle, like it might shatter if someone spoke too loudly.

Elijah felt it the moment he stepped onto the grounds.

Groups formed faster than usual. Not by grade or class, but by posture. By tone. By the way kids leaned into one another like they were choosing sides without being asked. Some whispered. Some laughed too loudly. Some stared straight ahead like they were daring the day to test them.

Tommy walked beside him, shoulders tight, rocking just enough to keep himself aligned. His eyes darted from face to face, cataloging threats the way he cataloged statistics.

"Elijah," he murmured. "People are... louder."

Elijah nodded. "Just stay close."

They hadn't even reached the building when the first comment landed.

"Guess the preacher man couldn't talk his way outta that one."

The voice was casual. Almost bored.

Elijah turned.

The boy leaning against the bike rack had a punchable smile and a haircut his father probably paid for twice a month. Clean clothes. New shoes. Confidence that came from never having been told no in a way that stuck.

His name was **Wade Carter**.

Elijah knew it because Wade made sure everyone did.

Wade wasn't the biggest kid. He wasn't the smartest either. But he had a talent for knowing exactly where to press. He'd been practicing it his whole life.

A couple of boys snickered behind him.

Elijah's chest tightened. "Shut up."

Wade raised his eyebrows. "What? I'm just sayin'. Everybody's cryin' over some guy they never met."

Tommy froze.

"Died," Tommy said quietly. "Assassinated."

Wade's smile widened. "Yeah? Happens."

Elijah stepped forward before he could stop himself. "You don't get to talk like that."

Wade straightened. "Or what?"

The old question. The one that never needed an answer because the people asking it were always hoping for one.

A teacher's voice cut in from the doorway. "Inside. Now."

The moment passed, but it didn't dissolve. It followed them into the building like a bad smell.

Classroom rules had changed.

Desks were rearranged again, tighter now, as if proximity might force civility. The teacher's voice shook when she spoke about respect and understanding, words she had probably underlined in her lesson plan as if that might make them hold.

Someone whispered behind Elijah.

"Why's he even here?"

Another voice replied, softer but sharper. "Probably feels guilty, or maybe it's because he's protecting his retarded friend. My dad says the schools are being forced to let the 'coons inside. He also says we should do a 'lil coon hunting soon, with a rope."

Elijah didn't turn around.

Tommy rocked harder now, hands pressed flat against the desk, breath shallow.

"Elijah," he whispered. "They're wrong."

"I know," Elijah whispered back. "Just keep count."

Tommy nodded, eyes flicking shut for half a second.

"Nine innings," he murmured. "Three outs."

That helped. A little. Recess was worse.

The playground felt like a proving ground now. Teachers lingered near the doors, pretending their presence was enough, and pretending they'd stop a real fight if one broke out. They would, but only if it was between two people of the same color. Otherwise, they'd turn a blind eye and pretend their presence alone would thwart anything bad from happening. It wouldn't.

Wade found them near the fence.

Of course he did.

"Hey," he called. "Hey, Numbers."

Tommy flinched.

"Coon boy," Wade continued, circling slowly. "Your friend here know how many riots happened this weekend?"

Elijah stepped in front of Tommy automatically. "Walk away."

Wade laughed. "Why? Afraid he'll start shakin' again?"

Tommy's hand slid toward his chest.

Elijah saw it.

"Tommy," he said quickly. "Eyes on me."

But Wade was already leaning in.

"My dad says y'all got what was comin'," he said lightly. "World's better off without troublemakers But he also said it's the first time someone's been coon hunting out in public like that in a looooooong time."

Something snapped.

Elijah didn't swing. He didn't shove.

He spoke.

"You don't know a damn thing," he said, his voice low and shaking. "And one day, you're gonna wish you did, but by that time your mommy and daddy won't be around to protect you anymore, and you'll get exactly what is coming to you."

Wade blinked, surprised.

Then his face hardened. "Watch your mouth."

A whistle blew from across the yard. A real one. For a moment, Elijah panicked, thinking his best friend had blown the whistle under his shirt. Sharp and shrill – the sound continued to cut through the tension in the air.

Teachers converged. Wade backed away, hands raised, the picture of innocence.

Tommy sagged against the fence, breath coming too fast now.

Elijah realized it was one of the teachers whistles, and he turned and grabbed his friends shoulders. "You okay?"

Tommy nodded weakly. "Didn't use it," he whispered. "I didn't."

Elijah felt pride cut through the fear. He removed his hands from Tommy's shoulders before Tommy could focus on the fact that he was being touched.

"That's right," he said. "You stayed."

Across the yard, Wade watched them with narrowed eyes, something calculating settling in.

This wasn't over, and Elijah knew it; Tommy felt it.

Because now there was a reason.

Not just skin.

Not just difference.

Now there was anger, looking for somewhere to land.

And Wade Carter had decided he'd found the perfect place.

12

The word landed wrong in the telling.

Elijah felt it the moment it left his mouth, even though he hadn't said it aloud. The children felt it too. They shifted where they sat, the porch suddenly smaller, the air heavier.

The oldest was the one who asked. He always was.

"Grandpa," he said carefully, "what does that word mean? The one you didn't say."

Elijah closed his eyes for a moment.

Some words didn't age. They didn't soften. They just waited.

"It's a word people used," he said slowly, "to try and make someone feel less than human. To turn a person into a thing so they didn't have to feel bad about hurting them."

The youngest frowned. "Why would anyone want to do that?"

Elijah opened his eyes. "Because if you convince yourself someone is less, you don't have to change yourself."

They considered that in silence.

"And who was Martin Loothur King?" she asked next, her lisp betraying her. "Why did everyone get so mad when he died?"

Elijah leaned back, the chair creaking beneath him. The hills beyond the porch were green now, finally awake. He smiled at her innocence.

"He was a man who believed you could fight hate without becoming it," Elijah said. "That scared some folks. It gave others hope. When he was killed, it felt like someone had reached into the country and torn something out that hadn't finished growing yet."

The boy's voice dropped. "Is that why the bully was so mean?"

Elijah nodded. "That, and because cruelty likes company."

"And Uncle Tommy?" the girl asked softly. "Why was he mean to him too?"

Elijah smiled, sad and fond all at once. "Because Tommy couldn't hide. And bullies hate anything that reminds them they're not as strong as they pretend."

The children were quiet again.

"Did you ever want to use the whistle?" the boy asked.

Elijah didn't answer right away.

He looked out at the trees, at the places where winter no longer lingered.

"Yes," he said finally. "Once."

They leaned in.

Then

The day Wade Carter decided to stop using jokes was the day Elijah understood how fast things could turn.

It was lunch period. The cafeteria buzzed with noise and metal and voices piled too high on one another. Elijah sat stiffly, eyes forward, counting breaths. Tommy sat beside him, rocking small and tight, his tray untouched.

Wade stood up on the bench across the aisle.

77

"Hey," he called, loud enough for half the room to hear. "Coon boy."

The word cracked like a whip.

The room stilled just enough to notice.

Elijah felt it hit him, sharp and hot, but he didn't move. He kept his hands flat on the table. He kept his eyes down.

"Don't," someone whispered. Not to Wade. To Elijah.

Wade grinned, encouraged. "What? He don't hear me? Or he too busy babysittin' the retard?"

Tommy made a sound low in his throat, a trapped animal sound that meant panic was already climbing him from the inside.

"Elijah," he whispered. "Too many. Too loud."

Wade hopped down, closing the distance between them. At the same time, Tommy stood up and grabbed his tray – he was going to bolt away.

"You hear that?" Wade said. "Your pet's about to start shakin' again."

Elijah stood.

Slowly. Deliberately.

"Sit down," he said to Wade as he stepped around Tommy to ensure Wade couldn't get to him.

Wade laughed. "Make me."

Someone shoved Tommy from behind.

Not hard, but hard enough.

Tommy stumbled forward and hit Elijah, tray clattering to the floor, milk splashing white across linoleum. He dropped to his knees, hands flying to his ears, rocking violently now, breath tearing apart.

The cafeteria erupted.

Laughter. Shouting. Someone chanting Wade's name like this was a game.

"Elijah," Tommy cried. "Please. Please."

Elijah's vision narrowed.

He shoved past the kid that pushed Tommy, and dropped beside his friend, pulling him close, shielding him with his own body as best he could.

"Radio," Elijah said desperately. "Tommy, think about the radio."

Tommy's hands clawed at his shirt.

"Elijah," he sobbed. "I can't. I can't. I want it quiet."

His fingers closed around the whistle.

Elijah saw it.

Cold certainty washed through him.

For the first time, the thought didn't scare him.

It tempted him.

If he blows it, Elijah thought, *everything stops.* No Wade. No cafeteria. No hatred. No fists. Just quiet. Just safe.

Elijah's hands shook.

He leaned close to Tommy's ear, voice breaking. "Tommy... if you do that, you don't come back."

Tommy's sobbing hitched. "I don't want this world."

Elijah swallowed hard.

"I know," he whispered. "But I do."

Tommy's eyes met his through tears.

"You do?" he asked.

Elijah nodded, even as his chest felt like it might split. "I want tomorrow. I want baseball games we ain't heard yet. I want you to ride that bike one day without fallin'. I want you sittin' by that fence when we're old and mean and still here."

The chanting faltered. A teacher shouted. Hands grabbed shoulders. Someone pulled Wade away.

Tommy's grip on the whistle loosened.

He collapsed forward, sobbing into Elijah's chest.

Elijah held him and shook, the weight of what almost happened crashing into him all at once.

Later, much later, as they walked home under a sky that didn't care what almost ended, Tommy spoke.

"Thank you," he said quietly.

"For what?"

"For not lettin' me go," Tommy replied.

Elijah looked at him, twelve years old and already carrying a lifetime.

"Yeah," he said. "Anytime."

And that was the moment Elijah understood something terrible and true.

Sometimes love doesn't look like saving someone.

Sometimes it looks like asking them to stay in a world that has given them every reason to leave; and choosing to stay with them anyway.

13

Elijah didn't want to go.

Not because he didn't care. Because he cared too much, and he knew better than to say that out loud. He sat stiffly in the back seat as his parents drove through streets he recognized and streets he didn't, past houses that looked the same and houses that had learned to look away.

The meeting was held in the basement of a church that smelled like old hymnals and floor wax. The kind of place that had heard prayers whispered and shouted, promises made and broken. Folding chairs were set up in uneven rows. A few men stood along the walls, arms crossed, guarding nothing and everything at once.

Elijah's mother squeezed his knee before they sat. "You listen," she whispered. "You don't interrupt."

He nodded.

He always did.

The room filled slowly. Women in pressed dresses. Men with tired eyes and careful voices. Young people clustered together, trying to look older than they were. No one smiled much. Grief had a way of flattening faces.

A man at the front cleared his throat.

"We all know why we're here," he said. "So let's not pretend otherwise."

A murmur of agreement rippled through the room.

"Dr. King is dead," the man continued. "And we need to talk about what that means. For us. For our children."

Elijah felt his mother's hand tighten around his.

A woman near the front stood. "It means we ain't safe," she said bluntly. "It means talk don't protect you from bullets."

A man shot back, "Neither does burnin' down your own neighborhood."

Voices rose.

Another man stood, younger, sharper. "Y'all act like Malcolm was wrong. Like he didn't warn us. Like he didn't tell us what would happen if we kept askin' instead of demandin'."

The name moved through the room like electricity.

Malcolm X.

Elijah had heard it before, always spoken with care, like a match struck too close to dry grass.

"He was assassinated too," a woman said quietly. "Don't forget that."

The young man shrugged. "At least he told the truth."

"And what truth was that?" an older man asked. His voice was calm, but there was steel in it. "That hate answers hate? That's the truth you want my grandson to carry?"

The young man's jaw tightened. "He told us to stop lettin' ourselves be killed polite."

A murmur of agreement answered him.

Elijah shifted in his chair. He thought of Wade Carter's smile. Of the cafeteria. Of Tommy's hands over his ears.

A woman stood near the back, her voice shaking but firm. "Malcolm spoke to anger," she said. "And I understand that anger. Lord knows I do. But Dr. King spoke to conscience. And that scared people worse."

"Did it?" the young man snapped. "Because it didn't scare the man with the gun."

The room went quiet.

Elijah's father stood then. He didn't rush. He never did.

"Y'all talkin' like these men were opposites," he said. "They weren't. They were responses. To the same wound."

He looked around the room. "Malcolm told us to defend ourselves because nobody else would. King told us to hold onto our humanity because it was the one thing they couldn't steal without our help."

Someone scoffed. "Tell that to Memphis."

Elijah's father didn't flinch. "I will," he said. "And I'll tell it to Dallas. And if I gotta tell it somewhere else, I will."

A woman near the aisle wiped her eyes. "My sister wants to leave," she said. "Chicago. Detroit. Somewhere up north. She says Texas ain't worth dyin' in."

Another voice answered, weary. "Ain't nowhere worth dyin' in."

"But some places make it easier," someone else said.

The conversation fractured then, splitting into smaller arguments. Stay or go. Fight or endure. Teach children to keep their heads down or teach them to raise them high. Radios and televisions were mentioned, how they showed burning cities but never the reasons they burned. How they played soundbites of anger without context, faces without names.

The argument didn't end with names.

It deepened.

A woman near the center of the room stood slowly, as if she needed the floor to steady her before she trusted her voice.

"Y'all keep talkin' about Malcolm like he was frozen in time," she said. "Like he didn't change."

A few heads turned.

"He did start out angry," she continued. "And who wouldn't be? But by the end, he wasn't preachin' hate. He was preachin' understanding. He went overseas. He saw the world. He came back sayin' white folks weren't the enemy. Ignorance was."

The younger man frowned. "That ain't what they show on TV."

"That's because that don't sell," she shot back. "They don't show growth. They show sound bites. They show the version that scares people. They talk about liberals and being liberated, and they get some white folk to stand up and try to talk for us, like they are doing some great deed. Malcom said ain't nuthin' more dangerous than a white liberal woman."

Elijah felt his mother's hand tighten again.

"That man was killed *after* he started soften'in," the woman said, voice trembling now. "After he started talkin' unity instead of separation. Ask yourself why that part don't get remembered."

Silence followed. Not a sign of agreement. Consideration.

An older gentleman near the wall cleared his throat. "Same reason we tell Rosa Parks' story wrong," he said.

Several people nodded.

"We act like she was just tired," he went on. "Like it was an accident. Like history tripped over her."

Elijah leaned forward.

"She wasn't the first," the man said. "There were others before her. Women who sat down and were dragged off buses. But they weren't chosen to carry the story."

A murmur moved through the room.

"We chose Rosa because she was respectable," the man said plainly. "Because she looks like what America wants innocence to look like. Because when the cameras turn on, it'd be harder to say she deserved it."

Elijah felt something cold settle in his chest.

"They needed someone the world couldn't blame," the man continued. "Because the world will try to blame us for anything if you give it the smallest excuse."

A woman near the aisle whispered, "Even then, they tried."

"Yes," the man agreed. "Even then."

Elijah thought of Tommy. Of his shaking hands. Of the way Wade Carter's words landed because the world had already decided which explanations it preferred.

"So don't tell me this is just about anger versus peace," Elijah's father said quietly, reentering the conversation. "It's about control of the story. Who gets to be seen as human. Who gets edited."

Heads nodded slowly.

A man near the back spoke, voice heavy. "They make us look like monsters," he said. "Then act surprised when folks treat us like ones."

No one answered him.

Because there wasn't anything left to say.

The room seemed to exhale all at once, the arguments settling into something sadder and heavier than disagreement. Reality.

People began to gather coats. To touch arms. To murmur prayers that sounded more like hopes than certainties. Someone mentioned curfews. Someone else mentioned sending kids to stay with relatives for a while. A woman cried quietly near the door.

Elijah followed his parents outside into the thick night air, his head full and aching.

The streetlights hummed. Somewhere far off, a siren wailed, then another.

"Are we gonna' move, dad?" Elijah asked.

"I don't know, son. But one thing is certain – no matter where we are – we will always be ourselves. Ain't no man changing that, white, black, or otherwise."

Elijah looked up at his father. "Why do we gotta be so careful?" he asked. "Why does everything gotta look right before it matters?"

His father opened the car door slowly. "Because the world's always lookin' for a reason not to listen," he said. "And it don't take much."

They drove home in silence.

Elijah watched the dark slide past the window, thinking about men who changed and weren't forgiven for it. About women chosen not because they were first, but because they were harder to dismiss. About how being right wasn't enough. You had to be acceptable too.

And sitting there in the back seat, twelve years old and already tired in ways he couldn't name yet, Elijah understood something that would stay with him the rest of his life.

History didn't just happen.

It was curated.

And if you weren't careful, someone else would decide which parts of you were allowed to survive.

14

Summer arrived the way it always did once school finally let go of you.

Not all at once, not with fireworks or ceremony, but with a loosening. The days stretched. Shoes disappeared. Time stopped insisting on being measured so carefully. The air smelled greener now, thick with sap and water and the promise of being somewhere you weren't supposed to be for longer than anyone would approve.

Elijah turned twelve-and-three-quarters that summer, which felt close enough to thirteen to matter. Tommy followed a month later. They talked about it like it was a finish line they were both pretending not to watch too closely.

"You gonna be lucky thirteen," Elijah said one afternoon.

Tommy frowned. "Luck is inconsistent."

Elijah grinned. "Yeah, well. So is life."

The fishing hole was Elijah's idea.

It wasn't really a hole so much as a slow bend in the creek where the water deepened and forgot to hurry. Trees leaned over it like old men with secrets. The banks were soft and muddy, littered with footprints that told you who had been there recently and who had learned better than to leave tracks.

"My daddy used to bring me here," Elijah said as they picked their way down the path. "Before work got in the way of everything."

Tommy followed carefully, stepping where Elijah stepped, eyes scanning for snakes and sudden drops. He carried the tackle box like it was a responsibility, not a toy.

"Water temperature's lower under shade," Tommy said. "Fish like that."

"See?" Elijah said. "You already know more than me."

Tommy shrugged. "Fish are predictable."

They set up near the edge, Elijah tossing his line out with a practiced flick, Tommy mimicking the motion in pieces. His cast was short, plopping into the water with more sound than grace.

"That's fine," Elijah said. "Fish ain't judgin'."

They sat side by side on the bank, knees muddy, radios forgotten for once. The water moved lazily, dragonflies skimming the surface like they were drawing invisible lines.

Elijah talked.

About birds mostly. Red-winged blackbirds and how they screamed at you like they owned the sky. About turtles that would sit so still on logs you'd think they were carved until they slid into the water at the last second. About how his uncle once caught a catfish big enough to scare his mama half to death.

Tommy listened.

Every so often, he chimed in.

"Kingfisher," he said once, pointing. "Dives headfirst. High success rate."

"Yeah," Elijah said softly. "He's brave."

Tommy considered that.

A fish tugged on Elijah's line suddenly, sharp and insistent. Elijah whooped and stood, reeling it in with a laugh. A small bass broke the surface, green and furious.

Tommy's eyes widened.

"Size eighteen inches," he guessed.

Elijah held it up. "Maybe in your dreams."

Tommy smiled.

Not the careful one. Not the half-finished one.

A real one.

Later, when the heat climbed too high to ignore, Elijah kicked off his shoes and waded into the water, letting the cool wrap around his legs.

"You comin'?" he asked.

Tommy shook his head immediately. "Depth unknown."

Elijah laughed. "I'll stay where I can touch."

Tommy watched him for a long moment, eyes tracing the waterline, the way Elijah moved easily through it.

Slowly, cautiously, he rolled up his pants.

He stepped in.

Just to his ankles at first. Then to his calves.

The water rippled.

Tommy gasped, then laughed, surprised by the sound.

"Cold," he said.

"Good cold," Elijah replied.

They stayed like that, Elijah splashing, Tommy standing still, hands out at his sides like he was balancing the world. When a minnow brushed past his leg, Tommy stiffened, then relaxed.

"Feels like... electricity," he said.

Elijah nodded. "Yeah. That's how you know you're alive."

They talked about nothing important and everything that mattered. About how birds slept. About whether fish remembered being caught. About how loud the world felt sometimes and how quiet it got when you found the right place.

When the sun began to dip, they packed up, fish released back into the water, footprints washed away.

Walking home, Tommy spoke quietly.

"Elijah," he said. "This was… good."

Elijah smiled. "Yeah. It was."

They didn't say anything else.

They didn't need to.

Because for that one long afternoon, the world had forgotten to be cruel.

And the boys, standing on the edge of thirteen, learned something just as important as endurance or trust. They learned joy.

And they learned it together.

That summer felt endless.

Not in the way adults mean when they say it, not stretched thin or boring, but full. Packed tight with hours that bent instead of breaking, days that forgot how to end on time. The boys did not know they were standing at the edge of something. They only knew that mornings came easier and laughter found them quicker than it ever had before.

They built a rhythm.

Some days started with baseball, radios crackling low before the sun burned the mist off the creek. They lay on their backs in the grass, eyes half-closed, listening to the announcers argue balls and strikes like it mattered more than anything else in the world. Tommy corrected them constantly.

"Wrong count," he'd mutter.

"Wind shifted," he'd add.

"Elbow dropped. He's tired."

Elijah learned to tell when Tommy was happy by the way the rocking disappeared without anyone noticing.

Other days were for the water.

Elijah swam. Always. He loved the way the creek erased heat and worry at the same time, the way you could dive under and come back changed just enough to matter. Tommy stayed where his feet could touch, but that line moved a little farther out every week. Knees.

Thighs. Waist. Once, he even let go of the bank entirely for half a second, arms windmilling, laughing and panicked all at once.

"I did it," he said, stunned.

"You sure did," Elijah replied.

"Don't do it again," Tommy decided.

Elijah laughed until his sides hurt.

They listened to music too.

Not loud. Never loud.

Tommy preferred it that way. He'd turn the radio dial slowly, careful as a surgeon, bypassing the songs Elijah liked, the ones with shouting and drums and voices that pushed too hard. When he found the orchestra station, his whole posture changed.

"Listen," he said once, eyes bright. "That's Liszt."

Elijah blinked. "Who?"

Tommy frowned, like the question itself needed correcting. "Franz Liszt. Piano. Complicated. Beautiful."

The music spilled out soft and layered, notes tumbling over one another like they were racing downhill. Elijah didn't know what to listen for, but he watched Tommy instead. The way his fingers moved in the air, pressing invisible keys. The way his head tilted, tracking patterns no one else could see.

"This one's like Bugs Bunny," Tommy added suddenly.

Elijah grinned. "What?"

"Rhapsody Rabbit," Tommy said. "Bugs plays Liszt. Air date November ninth, nineteen forty-six."

Elijah shook his head in disbelief. "How do you know that stuff?"

Tommy shrugged. "It stays."

They laughed a lot that summer. Not because things were suddenly easy, but because they had learned where to put the hard parts when they needed a break.

The hideout helped.

It was Elijah's idea originally, but it became theirs.

Just past the bend in the creek, beyond the fishing hole, the woods thickened into a small pocket where the trees grew closer together, their roots twisting above the ground like knuckles. Someone long ago had stacked fallen branches into a rough lean-to, forgotten by everyone except squirrels and time. Elijah added to it slowly. A piece of scrap wood. An old blanket. A milk crate turned into a seat.

Tommy loved it immediately.

"Hidden," he said, approval clear in his voice. "Quiet."

They went there when the world got too loud. When voices carried wrong. When the fence felt thinner than usual. Sometimes they went just because they could.

The rules were simple. No adults. No bullies. Radios low. If you heard footsteps that didn't belong, you froze.

It felt like safety.

Until the day Tommy didn't show up.

Elijah waited by the fence longer than usual, radio already warm in his hands. He waited until the sun climbed high enough to make the dirt uncomfortable. He waited until worry started tapping on his ribs like it wanted in.

"Tommy?" he called softly.

No answer.

He checked Henson's. The creek. The path they always took.

Nothing.

By the time voices started carrying through the neighborhood, Elijah's stomach had dropped into something cold and hollow. Mrs. Miller's voice cut through the afternoon, sharp with fear.

"Tommy!"

Elijah didn't think. He ran.

He found him at the hideout.

Tommy sat curled against the tree roots, radio pressed tight to his chest, Liszt playing so softly it barely stirred the leaves. His face was pale. His rocking was fast and tight.

"Elijah," he said when he saw him, relief breaking through panic. "I came here."

Elijah dropped beside him. "Everybody's lookin' for you."

Tommy nodded. "I know."

"Why didn't you tell anyone?"

Tommy stared at the dirt. "Daddy was angry."

Elijah didn't ask more. He didn't need to.

They sat there until the music ended and the radio hissed with static.

"Can I stay?" Tommy asked quietly.

Elijah swallowed. "Yeah," he said. "As long as you need."

When they finally walked back together, the world rushed to meet them. Relief. Anger. Tears. Mrs. Miller hugged Tommy so tight Elijah thought she might fuse him to herself. His father yelled. Then stopped yelling when no one answered.

That night, lying in bed, Elijah stared at the ceiling and thought about the hideout. About how even the safest places were temporary. About how the world had a way of finding you no matter how clever you thought you were.

The next morning, Tommy was back at the fence like nothing had happened.

"You okay?" Elijah asked.

Tommy nodded. "The woods help."

Elijah smiled. "Yeah," he said. "They do."

They didn't know what was coming. Not really. Not the shape of it. Not the cost.

They only knew that summer was theirs, and for that moment, that was enough.

15

We didn't know what was coming. We didn't know how life would change, the shape of things to come, or the cost it would have on all our families. All me and Tommy knew was that the summer that year was ours, and we were determined to never let it go.

Elijah's voice went quiet after that, like the words had taken something with them when they left.

The porch creaked as one of the children shifted closer.

"Is the fishing hole still there?" the youngest asked. "Or did it disappear?"

Elijah smiled at the question. It was the kind children always asked, as if places could simply wander off when no one was watching.

"Places don't disappear," he said. "They just stop bein' yours."

The boy frowned. "What about Uncle Tommy's house? Where was it? How'd he get here… to Arkansas?"

Elijah leaned back and let the hills fill his vision. The Ozarks were different from Texas. Softer, somehow. Like the land itself had learned patience.

"That," he said quietly, "is where the summer ended."

The children waited.

Then

Tommy's father left on a Thursday evening after the sun went down.

No shouting. No warning. Just a slammed door and an engine coughing to life before catching. Mrs. Miller stood in the doorway holding a dish towel she hadn't realized she'd grabbed, watching dust settle where her husband had been.

Tommy sat on the floor, back against the wall, radio pressed to his chest.

"He's not comin' back," he said.

It wasn't fear in his voice. It was math.

Mrs. Miller didn't cry right away. She sat beside him and pulled him close, rocking not because she needed it, but because he did.

The town talked. They always did. About what kind of man leaves. About what kind of woman gets left. About what kind of boy that produces.

Elijah's father heard about it before Elijah did.

That night, after supper, he cleared his throat and looked at his wife in a way that meant a decision had already been made somewhere deep.

"We're leavin' Texas," he said.

The room went still.

Elijah's heart kicked hard. "What about school?"

"What about work?" his mother asked.

His father rubbed his hands together. "Work'll be there somewhere else. So will school. But this place," he gestured vaguely, "this place is teachin' our boys lessons I don't want finished."

They didn't leave right away. Leaving never worked like that. It happened in pieces. A job lead through a cousin. A church contact who knew a man who knew a cabin outside a town so small it barely bothered with a name.

Arkansas.

The Ozarks.

Green. Quiet. Far enough away to feel like starting over even if you knew better.

Mrs. Miller made her decision the same week.

She stood at the Johnsons' kitchen table, hands folded, eyes steady. "I can't stay here alone," she said. "And I can't go north. Not with Tommy like this. I heard y'all are goin' somewhere quieter."

Elijah's mother didn't hesitate. "Then you're comin' with us."

They packed together.

Two families reduced to what could fit in trucks and boxes and hope. They left Dallas before sunrise, the city still asleep, still simmering.

Elijah watched it shrink in the rear window and felt something loosen in his chest that he hadn't realized was clenched.

Arkansas was different.

The woods closed in faster. The roads narrowed. Houses sat farther apart, like they'd learned to give each other space. For a while, the Johnsons and the Millers shared a small cabin near the edge of the forest. Too tight. Too many bodies. Too many memories.

But it was safe.

Mostly.

Black and white still didn't mix there. Not really. Folks were polite enough, but eyes lingered too long. Doors locked quicker at night. And sometimes, far off in the trees, there were lights that didn't belong to stars.

Burning crosses.

Elijah's father made sure the doors were barred those nights. He sat awake with a shotgun across his knees, listening to the woods breathe.

"Stay inside," he told the boys. "No matter what you hear."

They heard plenty anyway.

But for all that, those years were the best of their lives.

They found a new fishing hole, deeper and colder, with water so clear you could see fish thinking. They built a new hideout, smarter this time, hidden better, with paths only they knew. They learned the warnings of the Ozarks too.

"Gators don't care if you're brave," Elijah said once, eyeing the water.

Tommy nodded solemnly. "Or innocent."

They laughed more there. Harder. The woods swallowed sound the way Dallas never had. Baseball still played on the radio. Liszt still drifted through the trees on low volume. The whistle stayed tucked away, untouched, patient.

They were boys in a place that didn't love them but didn't hunt them either.

And that felt like freedom.

Elijah paused in his telling, the porch quiet again.

The oldest grandchild spoke softly. "Were you scared?"

Elijah nodded. "All the time."

"But you stayed," the girl said.

Elijah smiled, eyes shining. "Yeah. We stayed."

He looked out at the hills, at the land that had taken him in when the world grew too sharp.

"Because sometimes," he said, "the bravest thing isn't runnin' away. It's buildin' somethin' good in the middle of nowhere and protectin' it with everything you've got."

The children leaned closer; they'd forgotten it was still chilly outside. Grandpa was a masterful storyteller, and though they didn't ever meet him, they were enthralled at how brave Tommy was, and how brave their own grandpa was. After all, they were friends when it was still practically illegal to be friends.

Elijah cleared his throat to continue.

Arkansas had its own rules.

They weren't written down anywhere. They didn't need to be. You learned them the way you learned where snakes liked to hide and which roads went bad after rain. Slowly. Carefully. Usually too late.

The schoolhouse sat a mile and a half down a gravel road that never quite settled. White kids rode buses. Black kids walked.

That part was clear.

What wasn't clear, at least not at first, was where Tommy fit.

The first week, the bus stopped for him.

The driver looked confused, then annoyed, then resigned. Tommy climbed aboard stiffly, radio tucked under his arm, eyes fixed on the floor. The kids stared. Whispered. A few laughed.

It lasted three days.

On the fourth morning, the bus rolled past without slowing.

Tommy stood at the end of the drive, dust swirling around his shoes, watching it disappear like it had made a mistake and decided not to correct it.

Mrs. Miller went to the school.

She came back pale and shaking, lips pressed thin.

"They said he don't qualify," she told Elijah's parents quietly. "Said since we live together, he's... complicated."

That was the word they used.

Complicated.

Elijah's father clenched his jaw. "So what happens?"

"He walks," Mrs. Miller said. "Or he don't go."

Tommy listened from the doorway.

"I can walk," he said. "Distance is measurable."

Elijah stood up immediately. "So can I."

And that was that.

They walked together every morning, the gravel biting through thin soles, fog clinging to the trees like it didn't trust anyone yet. Tommy counted steps. Elijah watched shadows. They arrived dusty and sweating, already tired before the day even began.

The town noticed.

It always did.

The first thing left in the driveway was a dead crow.

Its wings were spread wide, pinned to the dirt with nails. No note. No explanation. Just a message that didn't need translation.

Mrs. Miller cried then. Quietly. In the kitchen. Where the boys wouldn't see.

The second time, it was words painted crooked and hateful on the fence line. Elijah's father scrubbed them off before sunrise, hands shaking, teeth clenched so tight his jaw ached for days.

The third time, it almost burned.

A bottle shattered against the side of the cabin late one night, flames licking up the dry wood before Elijah's mother screamed and woke the house. Buckets flew. Blankets smothered. Smoke clawed at throats and eyes.

When it was over, they stood in the yard together, coughing, shaking, alive.

No one slept after that.

Elijah's father took to sitting up at night again, shotgun across his knees, eyes trained on the tree line. Mrs. Miller brewed coffee that went untouched. The woods, once friendly, learned how to hold its breath.

Tommy's sister hated every minute of it.

Her name was **Susan**, and she was sixteen and furious at the world for expecting her to adapt. She missed Dallas. Missed her friends. Missed being seen as normal, whatever that meant. She blamed the move on her mother's bad luck and her brother's differences, and she didn't bother hiding it.

"I can't even bring anyone over," she snapped one evening. "They all think we're freaks."

Mrs. Miller didn't argue. She never did with Susan. She let anger burn itself out.

Susan looked at Tommy once, eyes sharp and tired. "You ruin everything," she said.

Tommy flinched but didn't look up. "Statistically unlikely," he murmured.

Susan scoffed. "God, I hate this place."

99

Elijah watched it all, heart heavy in a way he didn't yet have words for. He didn't hate Susan. He understood her too well. She had lost her world and been told to smile about it.

Time worked on her anyway.

Not fast. Not kindly. But steadily.

She saw her mother stand up straighter than she ever had in Texas. She saw the Johnsons take turns sleeping in chairs so no one was alone at night. She saw Elijah walk Tommy to school every day without complaint, without apology.

One night, weeks later, Elijah found Susan sitting on the porch steps, crying silently into her hands.

"He doesn't mean to be like that," she whispered. "Does he?"

Elijah shook his head. "No."

She nodded, wiping her face. "I know. I just... I didn't ask for this."

Elijah sat beside her. "None of us did."

After that, she stopped calling Tommy names. She didn't become gentle overnight. But sometimes she'd bring him water when he forgot. Sometimes she'd turn the radio down instead of snapping.

Forgiveness, Elijah learned, didn't arrive with speeches.

It showed up in small mercies.

The Johnsons and Mrs. Miller stayed.

They repaired the fence. They planted a garden. They learned which neighbors could be trusted and which roads to avoid after dark. They took care of one another the way people do when leaving is no longer an option and hate has grown loud enough to be noticed.

And through it all, Tommy stayed.

He walked. He counted. He listened to Liszt in the woods. He never touched the whistle.

Not once.

Elijah paused, the porch quiet again except for the soft rustle of leaves.

"That was when I learned something important," he said softly to the children. "Love ain't loud. It don't announce itself. It just keeps showin' up, even when the world's tryin' to scare it off."

16

"Grandpa," the youngest said suddenly, rubbing her hands together, "do you think we could have hot chocolate?"

The question floated there, gentle and ordinary, like it hadn't just stepped into the middle of a life being unpacked.

Elijah blinked, then smiled.

"That sounds like the best idea anyone's had all morning," he said, pushing himself up from the chair with a soft grunt. "Come on. Before your fingers freeze off."

They shuffled inside in a loose pack, air slipping away as the door closed behind them. The house welcomed them the way it always did, warm and solid and quietly patient.

Elijah moved by habit more than by thought. He filled the kettle. Reached for mugs. Set them out without counting, though he once would have. The children watched him with the mild fascination kids reserve for rituals they don't yet understand but already trust.

As the water heated, Elijah found himself standing still, hand resting on the counter, eyes drawn to the window.

Beyond it, the woods stretched dark and familiar, trees rising where they always had. Thicker now. Older. The land didn't remember everything, but it remembered enough.

The grandchildren didn't know.

They couldn't.

They didn't know that the brick walls around them had once been thin planks you could hear fear through. They had no idea that this kitchen had been one room once, crowded with bodies and borrowed courage. Two families had slept here together, listening to the woods for sounds that didn't belong. Two families, bonded by love and trust, and a belief in God that they tried their best to show everywhere they went.

They didn't know this had been the cabin.

Tommy's cabin. My cabin.

Their cabin.

It had grown over the years the way things do when you refuse to leave them behind. Brick added. Rooms expanded. Windows replaced. But the bones were the same. The floors still creaked in the same places. The air still held certain memories longer than others.

Good ones. Bad ones. All of them shared.

The kettle whistled.

Elijah startled slightly, then reached to turn it off, pouring the water carefully into the mugs. Powder bloomed into chocolate clouds, steam rising like breath on a cold morning. He stirred slowly, the spoon clinking soft against ceramic.

The children wrapped their hands around the mugs as soon as they were passed out, sighing in unison.

"This is perfect," the boy said.

Elijah chuckled. "That's what hot chocolate's for."

They gathered at the table, warmth settling in where cold had been. Laughter crept back in, quiet and easy. Someone burned their

103

tongue and pretended not to. Someone else blew too hard and splashed cocoa onto the table.

Elijah wiped it up automatically.

As he did, his gaze drifted again to the window.

The path to the creek wasn't visible from here. It never had been. But he could see it anyway, clear as if the years had peeled themselves back just for him. The bend in the trail. The tree with the split trunk. The place where the woods folded in just enough to keep a secret.

The hideout.

For a moment, he considered it.

Taking them out there. Showing them the spot. Letting them sit where he and Tommy had once sat, radios low, hearts quieter than the world around them.

The thought was tempting.

Then it wasn't.

Elijah smiled to himself and shook his head.

Some places didn't need explanation. Some memories didn't need witnesses.

And Tommy… Tommy wouldn't want anyone else there anyway.

The hideout had been theirs. Not because they claimed it, but because it claimed them. Because it had held two boys when they needed holding and asked nothing in return.

Elijah turned back to the table.

"All right," he said, settling into his chair again. "Where were we?"

The children leaned in, cocoa forgotten, eyes bright.

Elijah wrapped his hands around his mug, letting the warmth sink deep.

"Well," he said softly, "after Arkansas started feelin' like home… that's when we learned that even safe places can change you."

Outside, the woods listened.

And somewhere within them, a small, quiet place remained exactly as it had always been.

Waiting.

17

Numbers Don't Lie.

The thing about small towns was that everyone believed they understood baseball.

They talked about it like it was instinct. Like it came bundled with knowing when rain was coming or which dog belonged to who. But Elijah had learned early that understanding the *game* and understanding the *numbers inside the game* were not the same thing at all.

That truth announced itself on a Saturday afternoon at the county fair.

The field wasn't much. Chalk lines that wandered when no one was looking. Bases that rocked if you stepped on them wrong. A backstop patched together from wire and hope. But people showed up anyway, drawn by habit and heat and the promise that something familiar might behave the way it always had.

Elijah and Tommy sat on the grass just beyond the third-base line, radios pressed low between them even though the game was live and loud in front of them. Tommy preferred the announcer. The rhythm. The certainty.

"Elijah," Tommy said quietly, eyes fixed on the pitcher warming up. "He won't last."

Elijah glanced at the man on the mound. "Why?"

"Grip's wrong," Tommy said. "And his elbow drops on the third pitch. Every time."

Elijah watched. Counted. Waited.

The batter fouled off two pitches. On the third, the pitcher's elbow dipped just a fraction.

Crack.

The ball sailed deep into left field, bouncing hard off the fence.

People cheered. Someone cursed. Someone slapped a knee.

Tommy didn't react.

"He's tired," he said. "They won't pull him."

Elijah frowned. "Coach always pulls him after that."

Tommy shook his head. "Not today. Bench is thin. Score's close. He'll risk it."

The next batter stepped up.

"Elijah," Tommy continued, voice low, almost apologetic. "Runner's gonna steal second. Then third."

Elijah stared at him. "Both?"

Tommy nodded. "Catcher's late. Twice."

Elijah hesitated. Then he stood.

"Hey," he called, loud enough to carry. "He's gonna run!"

A few heads turned. Someone laughed.

The pitch came.

The runner broke.

Safe at second.

A ripple moved through the crowd.

Tommy leaned forward slightly. "Now."

106

Before Elijah could say anything, the runner took off again. The catcher fumbled the throw, ball skipping into the dirt.

Safe at third.

The crowd erupted.

Someone shouted, "Who said that?"

Elijah swallowed hard. "He did," he said, pointing at Tommy.

Eyes landed on him all at once.

Tommy froze.

A man in a faded cap laughed incredulously. "That kid?"

Tommy flinched, rocking starting up just a little.

Elijah felt heat climb his spine. "Yeah. Him."

The next pitch came.

A sacrifice fly. Run scored.

Exactly as Tommy had said.

The field went quiet in that strange way it does when certainty cracks.

"Well, I'll be damned," someone muttered.

The coach glanced toward them, squinting. "What else you got, son?"

Tommy's mouth opened. Closed. He looked at Elijah.

Elijah nodded once.

"Change-up next," Tommy said. "He shouldn't throw it. But he will."

The pitch floated. The batter crushed it.

Double.

The coach exhaled sharply.

A few minutes later, Tommy sat on the bench beside him, hands folded, radio gone quiet for once. He spoke only when asked. Short answers. Exact answers.

Elijah stood just off to the side, heart pounding so hard it made his ears ring.

For the first time, the world wasn't laughing at the boys, instead, it was listening.

When the game ended, the coach clapped Tommy on the shoulder. "You got a gift, kid."

Tommy nodded. "Numbers don't lie."

Elijah smiled so wide his face hurt.

They walked home that evening lighter than they'd ever been, dust rising around their feet, the sun low and forgiving.

At the fence just outside the cabin, Tommy stopped.

"Elijah," he said. "They saw me."

Elijah nodded. "Yeah. They did."

Tommy looked down at his chest where the whistle rested, untouched. "I didn't need it."

Elijah felt something settle deep and solid inside him.

"No," he said. "You didn't."

The fence stood between them, rusted and thin.

And for once, it felt like it might not matter at all.

18

The thing about being noticed was that it didn't come alone.

It brought friends with it. Expectations. Curiosity. Envy. The quiet kind of resentment that smiled to your face and waited for a better moment to show its teeth.

After the fair, people remembered Tommy.

Not his name at first. Just *the boy*.

The one with the numbers.

The one who called it before it happened.

The coach found them two days later, standing near the creek with their radios low and their shoes abandoned on the bank.

"You," he said, pointing at Tommy. "You busy tomorrow?"

Tommy stiffened, rocking once before stopping himself. He looked at Elijah.

Elijah shrugged. "Depends. You got numbers?"

Tommy nodded. "Always."

The coach laughed, unsure whether to take that seriously. "I need help keepin' stats. You think you can do that?"

Tommy's brow furrowed. "Define help."

Elijah smiled. "He means yes."

The coach squinted at him, then waved a hand. "Fine. Be at the field after lunch."

That was how it started.

Tommy sat on the bench with a clipboard too big for his lap, pencil moving in short, precise bursts. He didn't cheer. Didn't groan. Didn't argue with umpires. He simply watched. Counted. Noted.

"Pitch count's off," he said once, not looking up.

The coach ignored him.

Two batters later, the pitcher's arm dropped like it had given up the argument.

The coach exhaled sharply. "What'd you say it was?"

"Eighty-two," Tommy replied. "You wanted seventy-five."

After that, people listened faster.

Adults respected utility. They always had.

Kids… not so much.

Word spread through the school like spilled ink. Not loud, but impossible to miss. Tommy Miller, the quiet one, was suddenly important. He sat near teachers now. Near clipboards. Near decisions.

That made him visible.

And visibility had a cost.

Elijah felt it before anything happened. The way conversations stopped when they walked by. The way laughter followed a second too late. The way names were replaced with looks.

One afternoon, as Tommy packed up his papers, a boy leaned over his shoulder.

"You ain't even play," the boy said. "Why you get to decide?"

Tommy paused. "I don't decide," he said calmly. "I observe."

The boy snorted. "Same thing."

Elijah stepped in. "You got a problem, take it up with the coach."

The boy backed off, but his eyes lingered.

Later that week, Tommy forgot something.

Not a small thing either.

He wrote the same number twice. Paused. Erased it. Wrote it again.

"Elijah," he murmured. "That's wrong."

Elijah leaned over. "What is?"

"I don't know," Tommy said, frowning. "It should be right."

Elijah's stomach tightened.

"You sure you're tired?" he asked.

Tommy nodded. "Heat affects processing."

Elijah accepted that explanation because he wanted to.

The whistle stayed hidden. Untouched.

At school, a teacher pulled Elijah aside. "Your friend's very bright," she said carefully. "But... he needs supervision."

Elijah heard what she didn't say.

"He's fine," Elijah replied. "He just thinks different."

She smiled politely. "Of course."

That smile didn't reach her eyes.

By the end of the week, Tommy was a fixture at the field and an outsider everywhere else. Used. Needed. Isolated.

One evening, as they walked home through the trees, Tommy spoke quietly.

"Elijah?"

"Yeah?"

"Do you think they like me?"

Elijah didn't lie. "I think they like what you do."

Tommy nodded slowly. "That's different."

"Yeah," Elijah said. "It is."

Tommy reached up absently, fingers brushing the cord beneath his shirt. He stopped himself before touching the whistle.

"I don't mind," he said, not entirely convincing himself. "As long as you're here."

Elijah looked at him, at the way he walked a little straighter now, a little prouder, even as the world edged closer.

"I ain't goin' anywhere," Elijah said.

Tommy nodded.

They reached the creek just as the sun dipped low, light breaking through the trees in long, golden stripes. For a moment, everything felt balanced again.

But Elijah knew better now.

Being needed was not the same as being protected.

And the world had a way of punishing boys who stood out, especially when they did it together.

Still, as they sat by the water and let the day unwind, neither of them would have traded it for anything.

Not yet.

They went to the creek because it was the only place that didn't ask questions.

The water moved the same way every time, slow and patient, curling around stones that had learned how to stay put. Cicadas stitched sound into the air, steady and predictable. Even the warnings here were familiar. Watch the bank. Don't step where the mud turns slick. Keep an eye out for gators, even if nobody had ever actually seen one this far north.

Elijah liked to joke about them anyway.

"Just sayin'," he said as they settled near the edge, shoes kicked off, pants rolled. "You see somethin' with eyes floatin' where eyes don't belong, you yell."

Tommy nodded solemnly. "Unlikely. But possible."

Elijah smiled. "That's you all over."

Tommy sat with his feet in the water, toes curling in the cool. He stared down at the surface, watching ripples break apart and reassemble. His rocking had slowed, but it hadn't stopped completely. Elijah noticed the way his shoulders stayed tight, like he was bracing for something that hadn't arrived yet.

"You wanna talk about it?" Elijah asked.

Tommy didn't answer right away.

Finally, he said, "The number."

Elijah nodded. "Yeah."

"I don't miss numbers," Tommy said, voice flat. Not defensive. Confused. "They stay where they belong."

"You been workin' hard," Elijah offered. "Coach keeps you there all day."

Tommy shook his head. "It wasn't work."

He pressed his palms against his thighs, grounding himself. "It was... everything else."

Elijah waited.

"The crowd," Tommy continued slowly. "And the shouting. And the sun. And the chalk smell. And the way people stand too close when they're curious."

Elijah frowned. "I didn't even notice half that."

"I notice all of it," Tommy said. "All the time."

He picked up a flat stone and skipped it across the water, each bounce precise but weaker than the last.

"When it gets like that," Tommy said, "numbers don't disappear. They overlap."

"Overlap?"

"They stack," he explained. "Too many at once. Same as sounds."

Elijah pictured it then. Not emptiness. But crowding. A mind too full to move.

"So it wasn't the heat?" Elijah asked.

Tommy considered. "Heat didn't help."

Elijah exhaled slowly. "You scared me back there."

Tommy looked up sharply. "I'm sorry."

"Don't be," Elijah said quickly. "I just... I ain't never seen you doubt yourself."

Tommy stared at the water. "I didn't doubt myself. I doubted the moment."

That landed heavier than Elijah expected.

A fish broke the surface nearby, then vanished again.

"You think it'll happen again?" Elijah asked.

Tommy shrugged. "Probability increases with exposure."

Elijah's jaw tightened. "Then maybe you don't gotta do it every day."

Tommy turned toward him. "I like helping."

"I know," Elijah said softly. "I just don't want them breakin' you."

Tommy tilted his head. "I'm not breakable."

Elijah didn't say what he was thinking. That nobody ever thought they were, right up until they were.

They sat in silence for a while, listening to the creek. Elijah scanned the far bank out of habit, half-expecting to see something ancient and watching. Nothing moved but shadows and water bugs skimming the surface.

"You ever think about us leavin' again?" Tommy asked suddenly.

Elijah blinked. "Arkansas?"

Tommy nodded. "This place is quieter. But people are still loud."

Elijah snorted softly. "Yeah. Guess they always will be."

Tommy's hand drifted toward his chest, fingers brushing fabric. He stopped himself before reaching the whistle.

"I don't want to go," he said. "Not yet."

Elijah swallowed. "Me neither."

They watched the sun slide lower, light breaking through the trees in gold and green. Somewhere upstream, a log shifted with a hollow knock.

Tommy stiffened. "That wasn't water."

Elijah smiled faintly. "Relax. If there was a gator, you'd have counted its steps by now."

Tommy huffed, a sound halfway to laughter.

After a moment, he said, "If I mess up again…"

"You won't," Elijah said.

"But if I do," Tommy insisted.

Elijah met his eyes. "Then we deal with it. Same way we deal with everything else."

Tommy nodded, reassured by the certainty more than the words.

They packed up as dusk crept in, walking back through the woods side by side. Tommy's steps evened out. His shoulders loosened.

Behind them, the creek kept moving, indifferent to numbers and mistakes and fear.

And Elijah understood something new as they headed home.

The danger wasn't that Tommy might fail.

The danger was that the world wouldn't forgive him for it.

Still, as the trees closed around them and the path narrowed to something only they used, Elijah let himself believe, just for now, that this place might hold.

At least a little longer.

19

The first time Tommy spoke without looking at Elijah, it startled everyone.

It would have startled Elijah, but he was in the outfield filling in for a player that didn't show up to practice that day.

It happened on a Wednesday afternoon when the heat sat low and stubborn, pressing against the field like it had nowhere else to be. Practice had dragged longer than usual. The coach barked instructions that bounced off tired bodies, and the players moved with the loose impatience of boys who wanted water more than wisdom.

Tommy sat at the end of the bench with his clipboard, pencil tapping once against the wood. Not nervous. Thinking.

Elijah stood in the outfield, pretending not to watch him while watching him entirely, even from a long distance.

The pitcher missed the strike zone again. High. Wide. Frustrated.

The catcher groaned. "Come on!"

The coach rubbed his temples. "He's fine. Just needs to settle."

Tommy inhaled.

"Elijah," he started to say.

Then he stopped.

He looked up instead. Straight at the coach.

"No," Tommy said.

The word was quiet. Clear. It cut through the noise without raising its voice.

The coach turned slowly. "What did you say, son?"

Tommy swallowed once. His rocking started, then it stilled. His fingers tightened around the pencil, grounding himself.

"He's not fine," Tommy said. "He's overcompensating."

A couple of boys snickered.

The coach frowned. "You wanna explain that?"

Tommy nodded. "His shoulder's tired. He's changing the release point. That's why it's high. He'll miss the zone again. Then again. Then he'll hurt himself."

Silence.

Elijah felt his pulse in his ears. He didn't know what was being said, but he knew all eyes and ears were on Tommy.

The pitcher threw.

High. Ball three.

The coach's jaw clenched.

Tommy continued, voice steady now that he'd started. "He should be pulled. Or moved to first. He throws better when he doesn't have to think about velocity."

The coach stared at him for a long moment.

Then he sighed. "All right," he muttered. "Sit him."

The pitcher protested. The catcher blinked. A few boys muttered under their breath.

Elijah watched Tommy carefully.

Tommy didn't smile. He didn't celebrate. He just went back to his clipboard, pencil moving again, the world clicking back into its proper alignment.

Practice ended early that day.

Word spread fast.

By the next afternoon, people were watching Tommy differently. Not just with curiosity. With expectation. And expectation, Elijah was learning, could be just as heavy.

It came to a head during the scrimmage.

Parents lined the fence line. Kids crowded close. The sun dipped just enough to glare off the dust and make tempers short.

Elijah stood in the outfield, glove loose in his hand, eyes scanning. He caught movement near the dugout. Two boys whispering. One of them pointing.

Tommy stood alone near the bench, radio tucked away, clipboard resting on his knee.

The batter stepped up. The pitcher hesitated.

Tommy leaned forward.

He didn't look at Elijah.

"Curveball," he said. "Inside."

The catcher shook his head. Called for a fastball.

Tommy stiffened.

"Don't," he said.

The coach glanced back. Hesitated.

The pitcher threw the fastball anyway.

Crack.

The ball shot straight toward the outfield, screaming past Elijah's left shoulder. He dove, missed, rolled hard into the dirt.

Laughter burst from the stands.

The ground came up hard, knocking the breath clean out of him. The ball rattled against the fence as the laughter continued from the stands, sharp and unrestrained.

"Elijah!" someone yelled. "Get it!"

He rolled onto his side, sucking air, face burning hotter than the dirt beneath him. By the time he got back to his feet, the runner was already safe.

The inning dragged on for two more batters, but Elijah barely heard them. His ears rang. His chest ached. When the final out was called, he jogged back toward the dugout, head down, dust clinging to his knees.

That's when the shove came.

Hard. From behind.

He stumbled forward, catching himself on the bench just in time.

"Guess your little calculator ain't perfect," a voice sneered behind him.

A few boys laughed.

Elijah straightened slowly, jaw tight, fists clenched at his sides. He didn't turn around. He didn't swing. He tasted blood where his teeth had cut his lip.

Before he could move, someone stepped between them.

Tommy.

He crossed the dirt with quick, uneven strides, breath shallow but steady, and planted himself squarely in front of the boy.

"Stop," Tommy said.

The boy scoffed. "What're you gonna do? Count me to death?"

He shoved Elijah again, reaching around Tommy's shoulder like he wasn't even there.

That's when Tommy punched him.

It wasn't wild. It wasn't loud. It was clean and sudden and landed exactly where it needed to.

The boy staggered back, stunned more than hurt, hand flying to his jaw.

"You don't get to hurt him," Tommy said, voice shaking but unbroken.

The field erupted.

Adults shouted. Kids scattered. Someone grabbed Tommy's arm. Someone else hauled Elijah to his feet.

Tommy didn't resist. He didn't cry. He didn't apologize.

He just stood there, chest heaving, eyes locked on Elijah like he needed to make sure he was still there.

Elijah stared back, heart pounding with something fierce and proud and terrified all at once.

Later, sitting side by side on the bench, dust still clinging to their clothes, Tommy spoke quietly.

"I chose," he said.

Elijah nodded. "Yeah. You did."

Tommy's gaze drifted downward, fingers brushing the place where the whistle rested beneath his shirt. He didn't touch it.

"I didn't need it," he added.

Elijah felt his throat tighten.

"No," he said softly. "You didn't."

The coach approached them then, his face unreadable.

"We'll talk later," he said.

Tommy nodded.

As the sun slid behind the trees and the field emptied out, Elijah understood something that settled deep and permanent.

Up until now, he had been the one standing in front.

That day, Tommy stepped forward.

Not for himself.

But for the one person who had never asked him to be anything other than exactly who he was.

And that kind of choice, Elijah knew, changed the shape of a life.

Even if the cost hadn't shown itself yet.

20

The trouble with moments like that was how quickly they turned into stories.

By the next morning, everyone had a version. Some said Tommy had snapped. Some said Elijah had finally pushed him too far. A few said the punch had been coming for years, like it was fate catching up instead of a choice made in a single, clear instant.

Tommy didn't tell any stories.

He sat at the kitchen table that night with his radio pulled apart, pieces spread neatly on a towel, fingers working with careful precision. The music came through in fragments now. A note here. A hiss there. Static filling the spaces where melody should have lived.

"Elijah," he said without looking up, "the signal's wrong."

Elijah leaned against the counter. "You break it?"

Tommy shook his head. "No. It was fine earlier."

He adjusted a wire, then another. The sound improved for half a second before dissolving again.

Elijah watched him, a tightness settling behind his ribs. "You tired?"

Tommy paused. "No."

Then, after a beat, "Maybe."

That answer stuck with Elijah longer than it should have.

At school, the punishment came wrapped in politeness.

Tommy was told he could still attend classes, but he was no longer allowed near the baseball field. No clipboard. No bench. No numbers. The decision was delivered gently, like a kindness.

"It's for everyone's safety," the principal said, hands folded, eyes sliding past Tommy instead of landing on him.

Tommy nodded. "Understood."

Elijah didn't.

They walked home that afternoon through the woods, the path narrower than usual, shadows cutting across it like quiet warnings.

"I'm sorry," Tommy said suddenly.

Elijah stopped. "For what?"

"For causing trouble," Tommy replied. "Statistically, conflict increases risk."

Elijah stared at him. "You didn't cause anything. You ended it."

Tommy considered this. "Outcome was unfavorable."

"Maybe," Elijah said. "But I ain't hurt."

Tommy's gaze flicked up. "You fell."

"So?"

Tommy frowned. "You could have hit your head."

Elijah laughed softly. "You worry too much."

Tommy didn't smile.

At the creek, they sat without speaking for a while. The water moved lazily, pretending it didn't notice them. Elijah skipped a stone. Tommy watched it sink.

"Elijah," Tommy said finally, voice low. "Have you noticed... delays?"

"In what?"

"In me."

Elijah's stomach tightened. "You mean with the numbers?"

Tommy nodded. "Sometimes they arrive late now. Just a moment. But they arrive."

Elijah searched his face, looking for panic. There was none. Just observation.

"That happens to everyone," Elijah said quickly. "You been through a lot."

Tommy tilted his head. "It didn't before."

Static hissed from the radio, which Tommy hadn't realized he'd turned on again. He reached to adjust it, then stopped, hand hovering.

"Elijah," he said quietly, "what if the whistle isn't just for dying?"

The words landed heavier than any punch.

Elijah swallowed. "What else would it be for?"

Tommy shrugged. "Silence. Reset. Ending noise."

Elijah shook his head. "That ain't what he said."

"I know," Tommy replied. "But people are wrong sometimes."

The creek gurgled, indifferent.

Elijah leaned forward, elbows on his knees. "You ain't using it. Not for this."

Tommy nodded immediately. "I won't."

But he touched his chest without realizing it.

That night, Elijah lay awake listening to the house settle, to the woods breathe beyond the walls. Somewhere in the dark, a radio played faintly, music bleeding through static like a memory trying to stay whole.

Elijah thought about the punch. About the look on Tommy's face afterward. Not fear. Not pride.

Resolve.

He also thought about the hesitation. The tiny pause before the numbers came. The wire that hadn't been loose, but hadn't been right either.

Outside, something moved in the trees. A deer, probably. Or nothing at all.

Elijah closed his eyes and told himself the same thing he'd been telling himself all summer.

They were fine.

This was just noise.

Everything important was still intact.

But somewhere between one breath and the next, Elijah felt it.

The static wasn't coming from the radio.

It was coming from the future.

And it was getting louder.

21

By the time the leaves began to turn, school stopped pretending it mattered.

That wasn't entirely true. Bells still rang. Lessons were still taught. But for Elijah and Tommy, the shape of their days had already been decided. What remained was repetition. Endurance. Learning which fights were finished and which ones were simply waiting for better timing.

Tommy kept his head down after the incident.

Not out of shame. Out of calculation.

He spoke less in class unless called on directly. Chose desks near windows where the light didn't buzz as loudly. Teachers addressed him carefully now, as if they were afraid of setting something off without meaning to. He was no longer the curiosity. He was the complication.

Elijah stayed close.

They walked together. Ate together. Took the long way home when it felt safer to do so. Words mattered less now than rhythm. A glance. A pause. One of them slowing just enough so the other wouldn't feel rushed.

There were no more miracles after that.

No public victories.

No moments where a crowd suddenly understood.

Just small mercies.

A teacher who allowed Tommy to keep his radio low during exams. A coach who looked away when Elijah lingered near the field. A classmate who decided it wasn't worth the trouble.

That was how the rest of school passed.

Not with triumph.

With survival.

They still went to the hideout.

Just not every day.

It was still there, tucked back in the woods near the creek, branches grown thicker around it now, the blanket faded but dry. They visited when the world pressed too hard or when neither of them felt like explaining themselves. Some days they just sat. Other days they didn't even speak.

The hideout hadn't stopped being important.

They had simply learned how to carry it with them.

On the last day of school, they walked the path together as boys who were nearly done being boys. The creek moved slow and steady, unchanged.

"Elijah," Tommy said, stopping near the bank. "Why Arkansas?"

Elijah kicked off his shoes and dipped his toes into the water. "What do you mean?"

"Texas was dangerous," Tommy said. "But statistically... this place is worse."

Elijah smiled faintly. "Yeah. It is."

Tommy frowned. "Then why come here?"

Elijah skipped a stone. "Because we had family here. People who knew the land. Who knew which roads to take and which ones to avoid."

Another stone. "Because when trouble shows up, it helps to already know where it sleeps."

Tommy nodded. "Low visibility."

"Exactly," Elijah said. "And because sometimes it's safer to be somewhere folks don't bother lookin' too close."

They sat there a while, listening to the creek do what it always did.

After that, life sped up.

High school blurred. Jobs came and went. Elijah worked wherever hands were needed. Tommy found comfort in routine, in systems that didn't argue back. He memorized schedules. Learned the woods. Took solace in predictability.

They stayed friends because it never occurred to either of them not to.

They didn't talk about the whistle anymore.

They didn't need to.

By the time they were nineteen, the hideout had become something quieter. A place they went when words failed. When the world felt louder than it should. It waited for them without asking why they'd been gone so long.

By twenty-one, they were men in the way the world measured such things, though neither of them felt finished.

One night, sitting on the porch much like this one, Tommy said quietly, "Not everything breaks all at once."

Elijah laughed. "You talk like you're ninety."

Tommy smiled. "Numbers age differently."

Elijah didn't understand that then.

He would.

Because what came next wasn't gradual.

Wasn't patient.

Wasn't something you could outwalk or outthink.

It came fast.

And it came hard.

And when it did, it took something with it that neither of them had ever imagined losing.

That was when childhood finally let go.

And that was when the whistle, silent for so long, began to feel heavy again.

22

If you'd asked me back then what it felt like to be in your early twenties, I'd have told you it felt like finally getting your hands on the steering wheel.

Not because you knew where you were going. Because you were tired of being moved around by other people's decisions. We'd already been hauled across state lines once. We'd already learned that grown-ups could argue about your life like you weren't sitting right there in the room. So when things got quiet in Arkansas, when the cabin stopped feeling temporary and started feeling like *home*, it was easy to believe we'd earned something permanent.

We were wrong.

Not about home. About permanent.

That year, the woods were green early. Spring came on like it was making up for lost time, and the creek ran high from all the rain. The cabin felt smaller than it used to, not because it had shrunk, but because we had grown. Elijah Johnson, old enough to vote soon, old enough to work, old enough to stare at the ceiling at night and think about what kind of man I was becoming. Tommy Miller, a month behind me in age and a decade ahead of most men I'd ever met in the way his mind could snap a pattern into place like a trap closing.

We still lived there with my parents.

People sometimes hear that and think it was failure. That we never launched. That we never left the nest.

But that cabin wasn't a nest. It was a fort. It was a treaty. It was proof you could build something decent in a place that didn't want you to.

And it was the place that would hold us, long after we were done pretending we could hold ourselves.

Tommy and his mom lived there too, same as always. The cabin was a family that had been stitched together with necessity, then sealed with time. We split chores. We split meals. We split silence when silence was the only safe thing to split.

Susan had been gone for a while by then.

Tommy's sister left like someone escaping a fire. No note that mattered. No goodbye that held. Just a door closing and the sound of her footsteps getting lighter the farther she went.

Tommy didn't talk about it.

He didn't need to. I could see it in the way he stayed closer to his mother afterward, like he was replacing a missing piece without naming it.

And Mrs. Miller... she got quieter that year.

At first, it was the kind of quiet you don't respect enough. A tired sigh at the sink. A hand pressed to her ribs for a moment longer than it should have been. A pause before she climbed the porch steps, like she was calculating the cost of each one.

When I asked if she was alright, she smiled too fast.

"Oh, I'm fine, baby," she'd say. "Just workin' too hard, that's all."

My mama would look up from whatever she was doing and hold that smile for half a heartbeat too long, like she was pinning it in place with her eyes.

Then she'd change the subject.

Always.

Back then, Tommy and I had a name for it. We called it "grown-up business," and we hated it. We hated the way adults could speak in codes. We hated how they could make a room feel different without saying why.

But we also believed them, because believing your people is how you survive.

So when my parents started being... kinder than usual, we told ourselves it was just who they were. We told ourselves they were coddling Mrs. Miller because her husband had vanished and her daughter had chosen distance over family. We told ourselves my mama was taking her extra portions of food and turning them into extra portions of care.

We told ourselves my daddy fixing things around the place, more than normal, was just him being him. Hammering loose steps, strengthening door locks, checking the windows twice before bed.

We told ourselves it was love.

It *was* love.

We just didn't understand what kind.

Because my parents knew.

They'd known for a while.

They just didn't want to put the word in the air yet.

When a thing is named, it becomes real in a way you can't bargain with. And my mama and daddy... they believed in bargaining as long as there was breath.

Mrs. Miller knew too.

That part came later, when I finally understood how some people can carry fear with dignity. She didn't tell us. Not me, not Tommy. She moved through our days like she could outwork the sickness, like effort itself might shame it into leaving.

She started wearing long sleeves even when the day was warm. She started excusing herself after supper more often. She'd sit in her room with the door cracked, listening to the radio low. Sometimes it was music, the soft kind Tommy loved. Sometimes it was nothing but static, like she was waiting for the world to speak plainly and it refused.

Tommy noticed, of course.

Tommy noticed everything.

But he didn't name it either. He just adjusted around it.

He took her laundry before she could reach for it. He carried water without being asked. He started cooking breakfast on his own, not because he liked cooking, but because it was a pattern he could control. He'd make the same thing three days in a row if it meant her hands didn't have to.

One night, I caught him standing in the kitchen staring at the counter, unmoving.

"What you doin'?" I asked.

He blinked like he'd been somewhere else.

"Planning," he said.

"For what?"

He hesitated. Just a pause. Small enough you'd miss it if you didn't love him.

"For change," he said finally.

I laughed a little, trying to keep it light. "Man, you always talk like you're about to write a book."

Tommy didn't smile.

He just nodded once, like I'd accidentally said something true.

The first time Pine Hollows came up, I didn't hear it from him.

I heard it from my daddy.

I came in late from work, boots muddy, shirt sticking to my back. My mama was at the table with a ledger and a pen, her brow furrowed. My daddy stood near the sink, speaking in a low voice I'd learned not to interrupt.

"...they got rooms," he was saying. "Not just for old folks. Assisted living too. Folks that need help day-to-day."

My mama's pen stopped. "I know."

My daddy's jaw worked. "It ain't what I want."

"It ain't what any of us want," she replied.

I paused in the doorway. "What ain't what you want?"

Both of them turned so fast it was like I'd caught them stealing.

My daddy's face smoothed over into something neutral. My mama's pen moved again like it hadn't ever stopped.

"Just talkin' about… options," my daddy said.

"Options for what?" I asked, stepping in.

My mama looked up. Her eyes were warm, but there was a tightness behind them that made my stomach dip.

"For a friend from church," she said smoothly. "She's got an aunt that needs care."

I should've believed it.

I did believe it, sort of, because that's what I wanted. I wanted my parents to be talking about somebody else's problems, not ours.

But later, as I lay in bed listening to the cabin settle, I heard my mama's footsteps cross the hall toward Mrs. Miller's room. I heard the soft knock. The door opening. Two voices low enough to be prayer.

And I understood without understanding.

Something was happening in our house that didn't belong to anyone else.

The kindness got heavier after that.

Not louder. Just… more deliberate.

My mama started insisting Mrs. Miller sit while she cooked.

"Oh, Ruth, you just rest," she'd say, taking the spoon out of her hand like it was a child's toy. "You been doin' enough for one lifetime."

Mrs. Miller would protest, smiling, trying to keep her pride. "I can still stir a pot, Mary."

"I didn't say you couldn't," my mama would answer. "I said you shouldn't have to."

My daddy started driving Mrs. Miller "into town" more often. He didn't like town. None of us did. Too many eyes, too many questions. But he'd put on his best shirt and say he had errands, and she'd come back quiet and pale, moving slower than before.

Tommy and I thought we knew what was going on.

We thought my parents were giving her a break from loneliness. We thought they were trying to make up for Susan leaving. We thought they were trying to show Tommy that adults could stay, that abandonment wasn't the only ending men chose.

And I'll tell you something that still makes my throat close even now:

Tommy believed it was about him.

Not in a selfish way. In a frightened way.

One night, sitting on the porch steps with the cicadas loud and the air thick, Tommy said quietly, "Your parents are good."

"They are," I said.

He nodded. "They don't treat me like… a problem."

"You ain't a problem," I told him, without hesitation.

Tommy's gaze stayed on the yard. "Others do."

"Yeah," I admitted. "But they're wrong."

Tommy breathed out slowly. "Your mother is… consistent."

I smiled. "That's one word for her."

Tommy's mouth twitched. Almost a smile.

Then he said, soft as the night itself, "I will not waste it."

I frowned. "Waste what?"

Tommy touched the fabric over his chest, not fully reaching for what was beneath. "Mercy," he said.

I didn't understand then.

I would later.

The day the truth almost broke through was a Sunday.

Church had let out, and people were still lingering in the yard like they didn't want to go back to whatever waited at home. My daddy stood with a couple men, talking low. My mama was helping fold chairs. Mrs. Miller sat in the shade, smiling at folks, nodding like everything was fine.

Tommy was beside her, upright and careful, like a guard dog that didn't bite.

A woman from church came up and squeezed Mrs. Miller's shoulder. "How you holdin' up, honey?"

Mrs. Miller smiled. "I'm blessed."

The woman's eyes flicked to my mama. "It's good you got help," she said gently.

Mrs. Miller's smile held, but her fingers tightened on her skirt.

My mama stepped forward, quick and smooth. "We're all family," she said.

The woman nodded, then leaned in, lowering her voice. I wasn't supposed to hear it, but I did.

"Pine Hollows got a good wing," she whispered. "If it comes to that."

Mrs. Miller's face didn't change.

But Tommy's did.

Just for a second.

A crack.

His eyes sharpened, trying to pin the words down, trying to turn them into something he could measure.

"Wing," he murmured, barely audible. "Like… birds?"

The woman smiled awkwardly. "No, sweetheart. Not like birds."

Tommy stared at her.

Then he looked at his mother.

Mrs. Miller reached up and patted his hand, slow and gentle, like she was calming a horse. "Don't you worry about nothin', Tommy," she said, voice honey-smooth. "You hear me? Not a thing."

Tommy nodded.

Because he trusted her.

Because mothers are the first numbers boys believe in.

Later that night, after supper, after dishes, after the day had pretended to end normally, my daddy asked me to come outside.

We stood near the edge of the yard, where the woods started and the porch light couldn't quite push the dark away. My daddy's face looked older than it had a week before. He rubbed his hands together like he was warming them, even though it wasn't cold.

"You and Tommy doin' alright?" he asked.

"Yeah," I said. "Why wouldn't we be?"

My daddy's eyes stayed on the trees. "Just askin'."

I laughed a little, trying to lighten the air. "He's fine. He's… Tommy."

My daddy nodded, slow. "He's a good boy."

"Best I know," I said.

My daddy's jaw worked. "You know you can come to me if somethin' ever feels… too heavy."

I frowned. "What's goin' on?"

He looked at me then. Really looked.

And I swear, for a second, I thought he was going to tell me.

Then he didn't.

He just reached out and squeezed my shoulder, hard enough to hurt.

"Just keep an eye on him," he said.

"On Tommy?"

My daddy nodded. "On both of 'em."

I swallowed. "Okay."

He turned toward the house. "Go on inside."

I watched him walk back to the porch and pause, listening to the quiet like it might betray something. Then he stepped inside and closed the door.

And I stood there a moment longer, staring at the woods, feeling like I'd been handed a responsibility without being told what it was.

Inside, Tommy sat at the table with his radio, tuning it carefully to the orchestra station. A soft piano piece came through, smooth as water over stone.

Tommy's fingers moved in the air, pressing invisible keys.

Mrs. Miller sat in a chair nearby, knitting something she'd already started three times, her hands not quite obeying the way they used to.

She looked up at me and smiled.

It was the same smile she'd been wearing for months.

Brave. Gentle. Too practiced.

"Come sit, Elijah," she said. "It's a nice one."

I sat.

Tommy nodded at the music. "Liszt," he said, pleased. "He resolves."

I leaned back and listened, letting the notes fill the room where words wouldn't go.

Because that was the thing about that time.

The cabin was full of love. Full of laughter in small doses. Full of routine and supper and chores and quiet porch nights.

But it was also full of something else.

A story being prepared.

A storm being measured.

A truth being carried by adults who didn't want to drop it on two boys who had already been knocked down enough.

We thought the kindness meant we were safe.

We didn't know it was training.

Not for baseball. Not for life.

For grief.

And for the first time, even though I didn't have the facts, I felt it anyway.

That heavy, humming sense that something was coming.

Something you couldn't punch your way out of.

Something no numbers could predict.

Something that would make even the sweetest music sound like it was saying goodbye.

23

If grief had an opposite, it would look like that year.

Not happiness. Not relief.

Just the long middle stretch where nothing dramatic happens, but everything important quietly changes shape.

Mrs. Miller didn't collapse. She didn't waste away overnight. She woke up every morning and made it to the table and asked about our days like she always had. She folded laundry slowly, carefully, like each shirt deserved respect. She hummed along with the radio when the orchestra came on, even when she couldn't quite keep the tune.

If you didn't know what to look for, you'd think she was fine.

That's how she wanted it.

Tommy became her shadow.

Not in the way a scared child clings, but in the way a man measures distance. He stayed close enough to intervene without hovering. He learned her rhythms better than she did. When she tired. When she forgot words. When standing became optional instead of assumed.

He adjusted.

That's what Tommy always did.

"Elijah," he said one morning as we washed dishes side by side, "did you know people compensate instinctively?"

"For what?" I asked.

"For loss," he replied. "They don't announce it. They fill gaps."

I glanced toward the living room where my mama sat with Mrs. Miller, their heads bent together, voices low. "Guess that's just bein' human."

Tommy nodded. "Yes. But humans do it inefficiently."

I smiled. "You got a better system?"

He paused. "I'm working on one."

That should've scared me.

It didn't.

Because the cabin still felt whole. My daddy still came home at night. Supper still happened. Laughter still found us when it wanted to. And when things feel mostly normal, your brain fights to keep them that way.

Pine Hollows became a word we heard more often.

Not shouted. Not announced.

Just mentioned.

"Mrs. Jenkins moved there," someone would say at church. "They got good nurses," another would add. "It ain't just old folks," someone else would explain, like they were offering comfort.

Tommy listened. Filed it away.

He didn't ask questions.

He never did when the answers might arrive before he was ready.

The first time Mrs. Miller stayed overnight somewhere that wasn't the cabin, it was explained to Tommy as tests.

"Just a couple days," my mama said brightly. "They're bein' cautious."

Tommy nodded. "Caution reduces error."

He packed her bag himself. Folded clothes precisely. Labeled everything.

Mrs. Miller watched him with soft eyes. "You don't gotta do all that, baby."

"I do," he said gently. "It helps."

She kissed his forehead. "You always were my helper."

He froze for half a second, then smiled.

The days she was gone stretched oddly. Not empty. Just… thinner.

Tommy filled the space with routines. Breakfast at the same time. Radio on the same station. Dishes stacked the same way every night. He didn't speak much unless spoken to, and even then, his answers were shorter.

When Mrs. Miller came home, she looked smaller.

Not weaker. Just… contained.

She sat more. Walked less. Her smile came quicker, like she didn't want to waste it.

One evening, as the sun dropped behind the trees and the cicadas warmed up for their nightly chorus, I found Tommy standing on the porch, staring out into the woods.

"You okay?" I asked.

"Yes," he said.

Then, after a beat, "I am prepared."

"For what?"

He didn't answer right away. Instead, he said, "Did you know there's a phase in music where tension resolves, but the listener doesn't realize it until the next note?"

I frowned. "Can't say I did."

Tommy nodded. "That's where we are."

I didn't like the way that sounded.

My parents' kindness sharpened during that time.

My mama stopped asking Mrs. Miller if she needed help and started telling her when she was going to sit down. My daddy adjusted the house without comment. Grab bars in the bathroom. A chair halfway up the porch steps. Little things that pretended to be nothing.

I thought it was love adapting, and indeed, it was.

But it was also preparation.

The day Pine Hollows stopped being hypothetical came quietly.

Mrs. Miller sat at the table, hands folded, posture straight like she was about to be graded. My mama sat beside her. My daddy leaned against the counter. Tommy stood near the door, close enough to leave if he needed to.

"Elijah," my mama said softly, "come over here and sit."

I did.

Mrs. Miller took a breath. "I'm gonna be stayin' somewhere for a bit," she said. "Just to get stronger."

Tommy nodded immediately. "Temporary placement."

She smiled. "That's right."

"Distance?" he asked.

"Not far," my daddy said. "You can visit whenever you want."

Tommy calculated silently. I could see it happening. Distances. Schedules. Possibilities.

"Pine Hollows," he said.

The room went still.

Mrs. Miller reached for his hand. "Yes."

Tommy squeezed back, gentle. "That is... acceptable."

I stared at him. "You okay with this?"

He turned to me. "It makes sense."

That was the moment I realized something was wrong.

Not with him.

With how calm he was.

The first night without her, the cabin felt off-balance. Like a table missing a leg but still standing somehow. Tommy sat at the table long after supper, radio on low, Liszt filling the space where her voice had been.

"Elijah," he said suddenly, "do you remember the man with the whistle?"

My chest tightened. "Yeah."

141

"He said it was for when you were ready to go home," Tommy continued. "He didn't specify where home was."

I swallowed. "Don't start that."

Tommy nodded. "I won't."

He reached for the radio, adjusted the dial slightly.

Static hissed, then cleared.

"I'm not ready," he said. "But I am… reorganizing."

That night, lying in my bed, I listened to the house breathe. I thought about my daddy's hand on my shoulder months ago. About my mama's careful smiles. About how everyone seemed to be bracing for something without naming it.

I didn't know then just how long the long middle would last.

Years, it turns out.

Years of visits. Of slow goodbyes disguised as progress. Of a woman who fought hard and quietly and loved her son enough to pretend she wasn't afraid.

And years of a boy who grew into a man without ever letting anyone see how much he was counting down.

We thought the hard part would be the end.

We didn't understand yet that waiting was where everything important was being decided.

And that somewhere inside Pine Hollows, without telling a soul, Tommy was already learning the layout.

Not for his mother.

For himself.

24

"Pine Hollows?"

The word came out of my grandson's mouth like it was just another place. Like a park. Like a store. Like somewhere you went and came back from without changing.

I hadn't realized I'd said it out loud.

We were back on the porch now, mugs empty, the night cooled just enough to remind you winter wasn't finished teaching its lessons. The woods stood where they always had, patient and listening. The same woods that had raised two boys and watched them become men without ever asking for thanks.

"Is that where Uncle Tommy lived?" the oldest asked.

I nodded slowly.

"What kind of place is it?" another one said. "Is it like a hospital?"

I took a breath.

"That's what folks think when they hear the name," I said. "But it ain't that simple."

My wife shifted beside me.

I felt her before I saw her move, the way you do after decades of sharing space. She knew what was coming before I did. She always had.

"It was an assisted living place," I continued. "And a nursing home. Folks went there when they needed help with things most people don't like to admit they need help with."

"Like what?" the youngest asked.

I stared out at the hills.

"Like rememberin'," I said.

There was a pause. Kids are good at pauses. They know when to let silence do its work.

"Was that when Uncle Tommy got sick?" one of them asked gently.

I opened my mouth.

Closed it.

My wife reached out then and rested her hand on my arm. Not to stop me. To steady me.

"That comes later," she said softly. "What matters first is why he stayed."

The children turned toward her, surprised. They didn't often hear her interrupt my stories. When she did, it meant something.

She smiled at them, the same way she had smiled at me the first time I'd noticed her watching instead of listening.

"Before Pine Hollows was ever his," she said, "it belonged to his mama."

Their eyes widened.

"And before that," she continued, "there was a time when your grandpa almost made a mistake that would've changed everything."

I frowned at her. "Now hold on—"

She squeezed my arm. "Let me."

I leaned back, a little stunned.

Because she was right.

I had been there for all of it. Every day. Every night. Every quiet choice.

But she had seen it from the outside.

And sometimes that meant seeing more clearly.

She turned back to the children.

"Your grandpa met me right around the time everything started shifting," she said. "And I need you to understand something before he tells you the rest."

They leaned in.

"He wasn't choosing between me and Tommy," she said gently. "He was choosing whether love was something you divided... or something you carried."

I swallowed.

She glanced at me then, eyes warm and knowing. "You can pick it up from here."

I nodded.

But before I could speak, the wind moved through the trees, low and steady, like it was turning a page for us.

And I understood something I hadn't back then.

The story of Tommy and me didn't start breaking when he went to Pine Hollows.

It started the moment I tried to build a future that didn't automatically include him.

And that...

that was where love first asked for proof.

I didn't know I was about to meet my wife.

That's not false modesty or dramatic irony. It's just the truth. At that point in my life, I wasn't looking for anything permanent. I was working. Helping at the cabin. Watching Tommy and his mama. Keeping the world steady enough to stand on.

Love felt like a luxury item. Something you bought when you were sure you could afford it.

I met her at the feed store.

That detail always makes her laugh now, but it's fitting. The feed store was where farmers went when they needed something real. Not pretty. Not polished. Useful. Necessary.

She was arguing with the clerk when I walked in.

"I don't care what the label says," she was saying, one hand planted on the counter. "If it kills the chickens, I'm bringing it back."

The clerk looked relieved to see someone else. "It ain't killed any chickens yet."

"Yet is not reassuring," she replied.

I laughed before I could stop myself.

She turned, eyes sharp, then softened when she saw me. "You think that's funny?"

"I think you're right," I said. "Yet is a dangerous word."

She smiled at that.

That was it. That was how it started.

Her name was Margaret, but she told me not to call her by that name unless I was mad at her. "Maggie," she said, holding out her hand like we were sealing a deal instead of introducing ourselves.

We talked longer than we needed to. About weather. About work. About how small towns had a way of knowing your business before you did. When she finally left, I stood there longer than necessary, holding a bag of feed I didn't need.

Tommy noticed that night.

He always did.

"You're distracted," he said as we washed dishes.

I smiled. "Am I?"

"Yes," he replied. "You missed a spot."

I looked down. Sure enough, the plate was still dirty.

"Huh," I said. "Guess I did."

Tommy dried his hands carefully. "New variable?"

I nodded. "Met someone."

Tommy tilted his head. "Romantic interest?"

I snorted. "You always gotta say it like that?"

He shrugged. "Precision matters."

I told him about Maggie. About the feed store. About the way she talked, like she wasn't asking permission for anything.

Tommy listened. Asked questions. Appropriate ones. Distance. Schedule. Frequency of interaction.

"Do you like her?" he asked finally.

I didn't hesitate. "Yeah."

He nodded. "That's good."

At first, Maggie fit into our lives easily.

She came by the cabin. Sat on the porch. Helped my mama without being asked. She noticed Tommy without staring, which mattered more than most people realized. She talked to him like a person, not a project.

I liked that about her.

She liked me.

That part came quicker than either of us expected.

The problem wasn't that she didn't like Tommy.

The problem was that she *noticed* him.

She noticed how I adjusted my schedule around his needs. How I checked in with him before making plans. How if Tommy wasn't comfortable somewhere, I wasn't either.

One evening, walking back from town, she said casually, "You and Tommy are close."

"Been my whole life," I replied.

She nodded. "I can tell."

There was something in her tone then. Not jealousy. Curiosity.

Later, sitting on the porch, she asked more directly.

"Do you ever do anything without him?"

The question wasn't accusatory. It was honest.

I thought about it. About the cabin. About Pine Hollows. About the way my days bent naturally around someone else's orbit.

"I don't see it like that," I said. "He's just... there."

She studied me. "I don't think you realize how rare that is."

I shrugged. "Guess I never needed to."

The tension didn't arrive all at once.

It seeped.

A pause before she asked me to come somewhere. A look when Tommy interrupted a conversation without realizing it. A night where she asked me to stay longer and I didn't.

Finally, one evening, she stopped walking and faced me fully.

"Elijah," she said. "I need to ask you something, and I need you not to get defensive."

That alone made my chest tighten.

"Okay."

She took a breath. "Where do I fit?"

The question landed hard.

"You fit right here," I said immediately.

She shook her head. "That's not what I mean."

I waited.

She gestured vaguely toward the cabin, the woods, the path that led nowhere and everywhere. "You have a life that already feels complete. And I don't know if there's room in it... or if I'd always be stepping around something sacred."

I opened my mouth.

Closed it.

Because she wasn't wrong.

"I won't ask you to choose," she said quickly. "I won't be that person."

I swallowed. "I wouldn't."

"I know," she replied softly. "But I also won't pretend it doesn't matter."

That night, Tommy watched me pace the porch.

"You're agitated," he observed.

"She thinks I gotta choose," I snapped.

Tommy frowned. "Between what?"

"Between you and her."

Tommy went still.

Then he nodded once.

"That's inefficient," he said.

My chest tightened. "Don't say that."

"It is," he replied calmly. "You shouldn't have to choose."

"I ain't," I said firmly. "I'm not goin' anywhere."

Tommy looked at me for a long moment. Longer than usual.

"Elijah," he said carefully, "relationships require rebalancing."

I shook my head. "Not this one."

He stared at me. "You don't know that yet."

That was the first time Tommy took a step back.

Not physically. Emotionally.

Small things. He insisted I go out without him. Told me to stay when Maggie asked for more time with me. Adjusted his routines so they didn't intersect as much.

I didn't understand it then.

I thought he was being considerate.

I didn't realize he was already practicing how to disappear without being noticed.

And that almost cost me Maggie.

Because love, it turns out, doesn't just want devotion.

It wants honesty.

And it was about to demand it from all of us.

25

Death doesn't arrive the way stories teach you to expect it.

It doesn't crash through the door. It doesn't always announce itself with alarms or prayers or last words that feel scripted. Sometimes, it comes the way winter finishes, quietly, after you've already started noticing the light staying a little longer in the evenings.

Mrs. Miller began to fade the same way she had lived that last stretch of her life.

With dignity. With effort. With love held carefully, like it might bruise if handled wrong.

By then, Pine Hollows was no longer theoretical.

It was a place with a front desk and a schedule. A place that smelled faintly of antiseptic and lemon cleaner. A place where nurses spoke softly, not because it was required, but because they had learned that volume carried consequences.

Tommy walked its halls like he had been there before.

Not confidently. Precisely.

He learned the layout faster than anyone expected. Left turns. Right turns. The long way around when the short way felt crowded. He greeted the staff by name. Thanked them with exactness. Corrected them gently when they misspoke about his mother's preferences.

"She likes the window open," he'd say. "She prefers water, not juice. She listens better in the morning."

They listened to him.

I noticed that Maggie noticed.

She came with us more often then. Sat quietly during visits. Watched instead of filling space with words. I could feel her studying Tommy in the same way she'd studied me when we first met, not trying to judge, just trying to understand the shape of something.

Mrs. Miller's good days outnumbered her bad ones for a while.

On good days, she'd smile when we entered the room and squeeze Tommy's hand like she was grounding herself in him. She'd ask me about work. Ask Maggie about her family. Joke that she was getting a vacation she never asked for.

On bad days, she slept.

And Tommy counted breaths.

He never panicked. He never rushed anyone. He just sat close enough to intervene and far enough away to let her be herself.

One afternoon, as Maggie and I waited near the vending machines, she spoke quietly.

"He's... remarkable," she said.

I nodded. "Yeah."

"He's doing things most people twice his age couldn't do," she continued. "And he's doing them without asking for anything back."

I smiled, proud. "That's Tommy."

She hesitated. "Does he ever... fall apart?"

The question caught me off guard.

"No," I said immediately. "I mean—he gets overwhelmed sometimes, but—"

"But not like this," she finished gently.

151

I frowned. "Like what?"

"Like someone who knows exactly what's happening and refuses to make it anyone else's burden."

That answer stayed with me longer than I liked.

The end came on a Tuesday.

Not dramatic. Not sudden.

Just... final.

Mrs. Miller didn't wake that morning. Tommy noticed first.

"She's still," he said calmly, standing by her bed.

A nurse came. Then another. Then a doctor who spoke in the careful voice people use when they believe the truth might shatter something fragile.

Tommy listened without interrupting.

When it was over, he leaned down and kissed his mother's forehead.

"Thank you," he said softly.

I don't know who he was thanking.

Her? God? Time?

Maybe all three.

The funeral was small.

Not because she wasn't loved. Because she had lived quietly, and quiet lives don't collect crowds the way loud ones do. People from church came. A few nurses. Some neighbors who had learned to be kinder over the years.

Tommy stood beside me the entire time.

Didn't cry.

Didn't shake.

Didn't reach for the whistle.

He held himself like someone who had rehearsed this moment privately and wasn't about to miss his cue.

Afterward, Maggie pulled me aside.

"I've never seen anything like that," she said, voice low.

"Like what?"

"The way he loved her," she replied. "Not desperately. Not selfishly. He let her go."

I swallowed. "He always knew how to do that."

She looked at me then, really looked.

"And you," she said, "never once tried to make him different."

I shook my head. "Why would I?"

She smiled sadly. "That's how I know."

"Know what?"

"That you're the kind of man who understands love isn't about possession."

That night, back in the cabin, Tommy sat at the table with his radio on low, Liszt filling the room again. The same piece he'd played the night he asked me if the whistle could mean silence.

I sat across from him.

"You okay?" I asked.

"Yes," he said.

Then, after a pause, "I am… lighter."

My chest tightened. "You don't gotta be strong all the time."

Tommy looked up at me. "I'm not being strong."

He tapped his chest once. "I'm being accurate."

Maggie stood in the doorway, watching us.

Later, as we lay in bed, she said quietly, "I don't think he's steady because nothing hurts him."

I turned toward her.

"I think he's steady because he knows exactly what hurts… and refuses to let it make him cruel."

I didn't argue.

Because in that moment, watching the space Mrs. Miller had left behind and the man her son had become in loving her through it, I understood something important.

Tommy hadn't survived life.

He had *understood* it.

And in doing so, he had shown both of us what real devotion looked like.

153

Not loud. Not demanding. Not afraid.

Just present; and unshakable.

I didn't know if he was the immovable object or the irresistible force; maybe he was both.

26

I thought I was done talking.

That happens sometimes when you tell a story you've been carrying too long. You reach the part that still hurts, and your mouth closes like it's protecting something you're not sure you can replace if it leaves.

The porch had gone quiet again. The children sat wrapped in their jackets, eyes flicking between me and the dark beyond the rail, like they half-expected the woods themselves to say something next.

I stared out at the hills.

"I always thought Tommy was the steady one," I said finally. "The calm one. The one who didn't bend."

My wife didn't answer right away.

She rarely did when she knew I wasn't finished yet.

But then she shifted in her chair, the old wood creaking beneath her, and spoke gently into the space I'd left open.

"He was," she said. "Just not in the way you think."

The children turned toward her.

I did too.

She smiled at them first, the way she always did when she was about to tell the truth without softening it too much. Then she looked at me.

"Elijah loved Tommy," she said. "Everyone could see that. What most people missed was how much Tommy loved Elijah back."

I frowned slightly. "I know that."

She nodded. "You know it emotionally. I saw it structurally."

I huffed a small laugh. "Only you would say somethin' like that."

She smiled. "Probably."

Then she leaned forward, elbows on her knees, hands folded.

"Tommy was always preparing," she said. "Not because he was afraid. Because he was attentive."

The children listened closely now.

"When you first told me about him," she continued, "you described his mind like a machine. Precise. Ordered. But what I saw wasn't a machine."

She paused.

"I saw a man inventorying his life."

I swallowed.

She went on.

"He knew what he could give, and he gave it carefully. He knew what he couldn't afford to lose, and he protected it fiercely. And when he realized you were building a life that might one day ask him to step aside... he didn't fight it."

One of the kids frowned. "Why not?"

My wife answered without hesitation.

"Because he loved your grandpa enough to make room for him to be happy."

That landed heavier than anything I'd said all night.

I looked down at my hands, old and spotted and familiar.

"I didn't see it," I admitted quietly.

"No," she said kindly. "You couldn't have."

156

She glanced back at the children.

"Tommy was very good at disappearing in small ways. Ways that looked like kindness. Like independence. Like maturity."

She turned back to me.

"But from the outside," she said softly, "it was obvious he was practicing."

The wind moved through the trees then, low and steady, like breath passing over a mouthpiece.

"Practicing for what?" the youngest asked.

My wife hesitated.

Just for a moment.

"For being alone," she said. "Without ever making anyone feel abandoned."

The children absorbed that in silence.

I felt something loosen in my chest that I hadn't realized I'd been holding tight for decades.

"I always thought I was the one protecting him," I said.

She reached for my hand. "You were."

She squeezed gently. "But he was protecting you too."

I nodded slowly.

Because looking back now, with the distance age gives you whether you ask for it or not, I could see it clearly.

The way Tommy insisted I go on dates without him. The way he learned Pine Hollows before he needed it. The way he never once asked me to stay when he could see I was torn.

He wasn't retreating.

He was arranging things so no one would have to choose.

One of the children spoke softly. "Did Uncle Tommy know he was gonna get sick?"

I closed my eyes.

My wife answered.

"I think he knew something," she said. "Enough to be careful. Enough to be gentle with time."

She looked at me then, eyes shining.

"He knew his mind was his home," she added. "And he knew one day it might stop feeling familiar."

The porch light hummed faintly overhead.

I thought about the whistle.

About how it had never been about death at all.

It had been about control.

About choosing when you were done losing pieces of yourself.

I opened my eyes.

"He never told me," I said.

"No," my wife agreed. "He trusted you enough not to."

The children shifted closer, as if instinctively drawn toward warmth.

I took a slow breath and felt the night settle around us.

"Tomorrow," I said quietly, "I'll tell you what happened next."

They nodded, satisfied.

Because they didn't know yet that the next part of the story wasn't about loss.

It was about waiting.

And how some people love you so completely that they spend years preparing you to survive their absence.

Even while they're still standing right beside you.

27

The baby came early.

Not dangerously early. Just early enough to rearrange everything that had already been arranged. Early enough to remind us that life doesn't wait for you to finish your conversations or resolve your quiet worries.

I remember the phone ringing just after midnight, the sound cutting through sleep like a blade. Maggie sat up beside me before I even reached for it, already knowing.

"It's time," my mama said on the other end, voice steady but bright. "You better get movin'."

By the time we reached the hospital, the halls were alive with that strange mixture of urgency and calm that only exists in places where beginnings and endings share the same walls. Nurses moved with practiced speed. Maggie breathed through pain with a focus that humbled me. I held her hand and realized, somewhere between one contraction and the next, that my life had already changed shape.

Our first child arrived just before dawn.

Small. Loud. Perfect.

When the nurse placed him in Maggie's arms, I felt something in me settle and ignite all at once. Love, I learned in that moment, wasn't something you divided. It expanded. Made room. Demanded room.

Tommy stood in the doorway an hour later.

He didn't rush in. Didn't crowd the space. He watched first, eyes scanning the room like he always did, taking inventory.

"Weight?" he asked quietly.

I laughed, tears still sitting too close to the surface. "Seven pounds, two ounces."

He nodded, satisfied. "Healthy."

Maggie smiled at him. "You want to hold him?"

Tommy hesitated.

Just for a moment.

Then he stepped forward, hands careful, posture precise. He held my son like he was holding something holy and breakable and absolutely real.

"He's warm," Tommy said, surprised.

"Yeah," I said. "They usually are."

Tommy smiled faintly. "Good."

He handed the baby back to Maggie after a minute, not because he was uncomfortable, but because he understood limits. He always had.

That night, after we brought them home and the cabin filled with new sounds and new schedules and new exhaustion, Tommy made his announcement.

He waited until things were quiet. Until Maggie had fallen asleep with the baby tucked against her chest. Until the house felt full in a way it never had before.

"Elijah," he said, standing at the kitchen table. "We need to discuss logistics."

I rubbed my eyes. "Man, it's two in the mornin'."

"I know," he said. "This is when thinking is clearest."

I sighed and sat across from him. "What's goin' on?"

160

He folded his hands neatly. "I'm going to move to Pine Hollows."
The words hit me harder than I expected.
"What?" I said. "Why?"
He gestured vaguely toward the hallway. Toward Maggie. Toward the baby. Toward the future pressing in from every direction.
"You have new responsibilities," he said. "Increased noise. Decreased availability. Predictable."
I frowned. "That don't mean you gotta leave."
"I'm not leaving," he replied calmly. "I'm repositioning."
"Tommy—"
"It makes sense," he continued, voice gentle but firm. "Pine Hollows has structure. Quiet. Staff. I already know the routines. And you—" he paused, choosing words carefully "—you need to be fully present here."
I leaned forward. "You are family."
He nodded. "Yes. That's why this works."
I shook my head. "Feels like you're makin' a choice for me."
Tommy met my eyes. "I'm preventing you from having to."
That sentence sat between us like something fragile.
"You ain't a burden," I said sharply. "You never have been."
"I didn't say I was," he replied. "I said I was… extra."
I stood up then, pacing. "This ain't about the baby."
"It is partially," Tommy said. "Babies change systems."
"So do friends," I shot back.
He watched me calmly. Too calmly.
"Elijah," he said, "love requires spacing."
I stopped pacing. "Says who?"
"Says reality," he answered. "You don't remove load-bearing beams when a structure expands. You redistribute weight."
I stared at him.
"You been thinkin' about this a long time," I said.
Tommy looked away.
"Since Mama," he admitted quietly.
That was the only truth he offered.

161

And it was enough to hide the rest.

The move happened slowly.

Not dramatic. Not rushed.

Tommy packed methodically. Labeled boxes. Sorted what would come and what would stay. He left most things behind. The radio. The books. The little objects that had accumulated over a lifetime of staying put.

"Why not take more?" Maggie asked him gently one afternoon.

He smiled. "I already know where everything is there."

That should have bothered me.

It didn't.

Because every explanation fit too neatly. Because every reason made sense. Because the baby cried and needed feeding and Maggie needed sleep and I needed to be present in a way I'd never needed to be before.

Because life was loud.

And Tommy was quiet.

The day he moved in, I drove him there myself.

Pine Hollows looked the same as it always had. Clean. Calm. Predictable. The kind of place that promised order to people who had learned to value it.

"You don't gotta do this," I said as we stood near the entrance.

"I know," Tommy replied.

"Then don't."

He looked at me, really looked at me.

"You're happy," he said. "That's the variable that matters."

I swallowed. "You are too."

He smiled. "I am… sufficient."

He reached out then and squeezed my arm, just once.

"Room enough," he said. "That's all I ever wanted."

I watched him walk inside.

I told myself he was right.

I told myself this was growth – Independence; love making room. I didn't know I had just agreed to the quietest lie of my life.

Because what Tommy never said; what he never needed to say - was that he wasn't moving to Pine Hollows for comfort.

He was moving there because he recognized the signs, and because he loved me enough to step out of the way before I ever noticed that he was beginning to disappear.

We would see one another frequently at first, and then less frequently, up until my parents passed away. My father passed first, and over that next year Tommy was around more often, stepping out of his comfort zone to help with our first child.

My mother passed just over a year later, right before the birth of our second child, and though it was loud in our home, Tommy was there to help as best he could. I never realized how hard that must've been for him, to deal with the variables that only he saw, all the while knowing what was going on inside his own mind and not placing that burden on anyone else.

Tommy was, without a doubt, not just the best friend someone could have, but the best friend anyone could have hoped for. I wouldn't realize that for years to come as life became busier and busier, but now I understand why life is so fleeting, and why Tommy did things the way he did them.

28

If you were looking for a sign that something was wrong, those years would've fooled you.

They fooled me.

Life didn't fracture after Tommy moved to Pine Hollows. It smoothed out. Settled into something almost elegant in its predictability. The place did exactly what it promised to do, and Tommy fit into it the way he fit into most systems once he understood the rules.

He woke at the same time every morning. Ate the same breakfast unless given a reason not to. Walked the same route through the halls, counting steps without moving his lips. He knew which nurses worked which shifts. Which ones talked too much. Which ones needed clear instructions and which ones preferred suggestions.

They liked him there.

That mattered more than most people realize.

Some residents were lonely in loud ways. Some were lonely in quiet ones. Tommy existed alongside them without intruding, a calm presence who could answer questions staff didn't have time for and notice patterns no one else thought to look for.

"Elijah," one of the nurses told me once, smiling, "your friend's got half this place memorized."

I laughed. "That's just how his brain works."

She nodded. "Wish mine did."

I visited when I could.

At first, it was every few days. Then every week. Then whenever life slowed down enough to remind me I hadn't been in a while. Tommy never commented on the gaps. Never asked for more. When I showed up, he greeted me like no time had passed.

"Score?" he'd ask immediately, meaning baseball, always baseball.

"Which game?" I'd reply.

He'd tell me. Date. Team. Pitcher. Outcome.

He was almost always right.

We'd sit in the common room or outside when the weather cooperated, radios low between us. Liszt still calmed him. Baseball still anchored him. Routine still held.

That was the lie.

Not a cruel one. Just an incomplete one.

From the outside, Pine Hollows looked like success. From the inside, it felt like relief. Tommy didn't have to navigate noise unless he chose to. He didn't have to improvise through chaos. The world arrived in measured doses, and he could respond on his own terms.

Maggie noticed first that I worried less.

"You seem lighter when you come back from there," she said once, rocking our second child to sleep. "Like you know he's okay."

"He is," I said. "This place suits him."

She studied my face. "It does."

There was something in her tone I didn't unpack at the time.

The kids grew.

Our house got louder. Toys multiplied. Schedules overlapped. Sleep became optional. I learned that love doesn't get quieter as it grows; it just learns to coexist with exhaustion.

Tommy visited when he could.

He never stayed long.

He'd sit on the floor with the kids, observing first, then engaging in small, precise ways. He liked stacking blocks. Lining them up by color. Counting them twice, just to be sure.

"Why Uncle Tommy count so much?" one of them asked once.

"Because numbers don't change," I said.

Tommy looked up at me then. Just for a second. Then he went back to counting.

After my parents passed, Pine Hollows became the center point instead of the edge. The cabin felt emptier, even with children filling it. Tommy came more often during that stretch, pushing past his preference for quiet because grief doesn't respect sensory limits.

He never complained, but I saw the cost.

The way his hands shook slightly after too much noise. The way he stepped outside to breathe when conversations overlapped. The way he sat perfectly still when overwhelmed, like motion itself might make something spill.

I thought it was grief.

It was, but it was more than just grief.

Years moved forward the way they always do, one ordinary decision at a time. Birthdays. Holidays. Ball games. Doctor visits. Small arguments that mattered less once sleep returned.

Tommy remained… stable.

That's the word everyone used.

"How's Tommy doin'?" folks would ask.

"He's stable," I'd reply.

And I believed it, because he still remembered baseball stats. Still corrected me when I got one wrong. Still hummed along to Liszt under his breath. Still recognized me instantly when I walked into a room.

Because nothing obvious had been taken yet.

There were small things, though. Moments that didn't quite fit.

Once, he paused before answering a question he'd never paused for before. Another time, he asked me to repeat something simple. He laughed it off, as did I.

"Long day," he'd say.

"Yeah," I'd agree. "Me too."

We were both telling the truth.

The whistle stayed where it always had.

Unused. Untouched. Not forgotten but not tempting either. It existed the way some promises do, acknowledged but deferred.

Life was working.

That's what I told myself. That's what everyone told themselves.

And maybe, in its own way, it was, because those years gave us something precious without announcing it.

Time.

Time to believe we were safe. Time to think we'd found a balance. Time to love without urgency.

Time, as it turns out, is generous right up until the moment it isn't, and by the time I noticed the difference, by the time the pauses lasted just a little too long and the corrections stopped coming as quickly - the plan Tommy had kept inside to himself for decades was already far ahead of me.

The *years* had worked.

That was the problem.

29

The first time someone said it out loud, I didn't hear it.

Not really.

It happened in a room that smelled like disinfectant and burnt coffee, the kind of place where chairs are designed for waiting, not comfort. A doctor sat across from me with a folder open, pages clipped together like that alone might keep them from drifting apart.

Tommy sat beside me.

Hands folded.

Back straight.

Eyes attentive.

The doctor spoke carefully. Too carefully. The way people do when they believe precision will soften impact.

"…cognitive changes…"

"…progressive…"

"…memory-related…"

I nodded at the right places. Asked questions I thought I was supposed to ask. Tommy listened like he was being briefed on weather patterns instead of his own future.

Then the doctor said the word.

Alzheimer's.

It landed between us without sound.

I waited for something in me to react. Fear. Anger. Denial. Something loud enough to prove I understood what had just happened.

Nothing came.

Instead, I felt the strangest sensation. Recognition.

Not *this is new*.

But *this fits*.

I turned toward Tommy, expecting confusion. Panic. Anything.

He was calm.

Too calm.

"How long?" Tommy asked.

The doctor hesitated. "It's difficult to say. Early stages can last years. Sometimes longer."

Tommy nodded. "That aligns."

"With what?" I asked sharply.

He looked at me then.

Really looked at me.

"With patterns," he said.

The doctor cleared his throat. "Many people don't realize what's happening at first. Symptoms are often attributed to stress, grief, aging—"

"I realized," Tommy said gently.

The room went quiet.

"When?" I asked.

He considered the question, not because he didn't know the answer, but because he was deciding how much of it I could carry.

"A while ago," he said finally.

"How long is 'a while'?" I pressed.

Tommy glanced toward the window. Sunlight filtered in, too bright for the weight of the moment.

"Before Pine Hollows," he said.

My chest tightened.

"You knew," I whispered.

"Yes."

"And you didn't tell me?"

He turned back to me. "You had children."

"That ain't an answer."

"It is," he replied softly.

The doctor shifted uncomfortably, sensing this conversation didn't belong to him anymore. He excused himself with practiced efficiency, leaving the door ajar like we might need help standing afterward.

I didn't look away from Tommy.

"You planned this," I said. Not accusing. Just stunned.

Tommy nodded once. "Planning reduces harm."

"You moved out," I said. "You stepped back. You let me think…"

"I let you live," he corrected gently.

My voice cracked. "You didn't get to decide that alone."

Tommy's expression softened. "I didn't decide alone. I decided *for you.*"

Anger flared then. Real anger. Hot and sudden.

"You don't get to disappear on me," I said. "Not after everything."

"I'm not disappearing," he replied. "I'm transitioning."

I laughed bitterly. "You always gotta dress it up in logic."

He smiled faintly. "Logic is how I survive emotion."

I stood and paced the small room, hands shaking. Every memory from the last twenty years began rearranging in my mind, snapping into a pattern I hadn't wanted to see.

Pine Hollows.

The stepping back.

The careful distance.

The way he never asked me to stay.

"You knew this would happen," I said.

"Yes."

"And you still—" I swallowed hard "—you still let me think it was about space. About the kids. About life."

Tommy's voice was quiet but steady. "Because it was."

I stopped pacing.

"What do you mean?"

"You needed those reasons," he said. "You needed a story that let you go forward without guilt."

Tears burned hot behind my eyes. "And what about you?"

He shrugged slightly. "I needed predictability."

The truth settled in then, heavy and irreversible.

Tommy hadn't just accepted his diagnosis. He had built a life around it long before anyone named it.

"How long you think you got?" I asked. He hesitated. That was new.

"I don't know," he said honestly. "Years. Possibly many."

I sat down hard in the chair.

"And the whistle?" I asked quietly.

Tommy's eyes flicked, just briefly, to his chest. "Not yet," he said. "That's for when I can't measure myself anymore."

The room felt smaller.

"I don't want you to do this alone," I said.

"I won't," he replied. "You'll visit. You'll remember me accurately. That matters."

My throat tightened. "You should've told me."

Tommy nodded. "Yes."

"Why didn't you?"

He leaned forward slightly, lowering his voice.

"Because if I told you," he said, "you would've stayed too close. You would've watched every mistake. You would've tried to save me from myself."

I didn't deny it.

"And I didn't want my last clear years," he continued, "to be spent reassuring you."

That broke me.

I put my face in my hands and let the sound out before I could stop it. Years of trust and love and shared silence collapsed into that one moment.

Tommy waited. He always waited.

When I looked up, eyes burning, he said quietly, "You gave me a childhood where I was seen. I'm giving you an adulthood where you don't have to watch me fade."

I shook my head. "That ain't fair."

He smiled, gentle and certain. "Neither was the world, but we adapted."

We sat there a long time after that.

Not talking.

Just existing in the space where truth finally lived.

Later, when I told Maggie, she didn't gasp. She didn't cry right away.

She nodded slowly.

"That explains everything," she said.

"What?" I asked.

"Why he's always been so careful with time," she replied. "Why he's never wasted a day."

I thought about all the moments I'd mistaken for distance.

They weren't distance.

They were gifts.

Tommy didn't lose his mind suddenly.

He gave it away slowly, deliberately, with love guiding every step.

And once the name was spoken, once the shape of the thing could no longer be avoided, I understood something that took me years to forgive myself for not seeing sooner.

Tommy wasn't afraid of dying.

He was afraid of forgetting who he had been, and he trusted me enough to remember him whole when he no longer could.

30

The strange thing about knowing is that it doesn't arrive with instructions.

Once the name had been spoken, once it had settled into the corners of every memory like dust you couldn't wipe away, life didn't stop. Tommy didn't suddenly become someone else. Pine Hollows didn't darken. The halls didn't grow quieter out of respect for what was coming.

If anything, everything sharpened.

Colors felt brighter. Sounds cleaner. Time behaved differently, stretching in some places and collapsing in others, like it was trying to decide which side it was on.

Tommy called me early one morning.

That alone made my chest tighten. He rarely called first.

"Elijah," he said, voice steady. "Today is optimal."

"For what?" I asked, already sitting up.

"For clarity," he replied. "The weather is acceptable. My head is…
aligned."

I didn't ask questions. I grabbed my keys, a light jacket, and I drove.

When I arrived, he was waiting outside, jacket zipped neatly, radio
tucked under his arm like we were boys again sneaking off to the creek.
The nurses smiled at us like they knew something important was
happening but didn't want to disturb it.

"You ready?" I asked.

Tommy nodded. "Yes."

We didn't go far.

Just a park on the edge of town. A place with benches and trees
and a baseball diamond that hadn't seen a real game in years. The grass
was patchy. The bleachers creaked when we sat down.

Perfect.

Tommy closed his eyes and tilted his face toward the sun.

"It's warm," he said.

"Spring's stubborn," I replied. "Always comes back."

He smiled faintly. "That's good."

We sat in silence for a while, listening to distant traffic and birds
that didn't care about timelines or diagnoses. Eventually, Tommy
turned toward the field.

"April 14, 1959," he said suddenly.

I grinned. "You ain't lost it yet."

"Milwaukee Braves versus Los Angeles Dodgers," he continued.
"Hank Aaron. Two home runs."

I laughed. "Still got it."

He nodded, satisfied. "Still do."

We talked then. Really talked.

Not about Alzheimer's. Not about Pine Hollows. Not about the
whistle.

We talked about the fence that used to divide us. About radios
crackling late at night. About the creek and the hideout and how we
never did see a gator, no matter how hard we looked.

"Elijah," he said quietly, "do you remember the man?"

175

I stiffened. "Yeah."

"He was accurate," Tommy said. "About readiness."

I swallowed. "You ain't there."

"No," he agreed. "But one day I will be."

He reached into his shirt then and pulled the whistle out.

I hadn't seen it in years.

It looked smaller than I remembered.

He held it for a moment, just looking at it, then placed it gently into my hand.

"Keep it," he said.

My fingers curled around it instinctively. "What if you need it?"

He shook his head. "If I need it, I won't know."

That hurt more than anything he'd said before.

We sat there until the sun dipped low and the shadows stretched long across the field. When it was time to go back, Tommy stood carefully, steadying himself for just a second longer than necessary.

I noticed.

He noticed that I noticed.

We didn't comment.

Before we returned, we made one more stop. We went to the cabin where we'd spent most of our lives, and while my wife and kids were inside, we snuck out behind the house and down the path to our old hideout.

"It's still there," he said as we moved the tattered blanket away from the entrance.

He was right – it was still there, and that "it" was our names, carved into a tree trunk, with the date. A constant reminder of the past. A reminder that hurts to think about.

After a bit, we headed back into town.

At Pine Hollows, before he went inside, he turned to me.

"Thank you," he said.

"For what?"

"For remembering me while I'm still here."

I pulled him into a hug then. Tight. Fierce. Unapologetic.

He hugged me back.

Fully.

That was the last day he was entirely himself.

I didn't know it at the time. None of us ever do.

But looking back now, sitting on this porch with the whistle heavy in my pocket and the night settling around me like an old friend, I understand how rare that day was.

It wasn't dramatic.

It wasn't loud.

It was just two old friends sitting in the sun, talking about baseball and birds and a world that never quite made room for them, but somehow never managed to take them apart either.

The last clear day doesn't announce itself.

It just happens.

And if you're lucky,
if you're paying attention,
you realize later
that you were given a gift
you didn't know how to ask for.

31

Decline doesn't announce itself the way diagnosis does.

It doesn't arrive with paperwork or careful language or a room that smells like coffee gone cold. It arrives sideways. In fragments. In moments so small you can miss them if you're not watching closely, and even if you are, you spend a long time convincing yourself they don't mean what you think they mean.

Tommy forgot a nurse's name first.

Not the face. Not the role. Just the name. He compensated immediately, the way he always had.

"You," he said politely, smiling, gesturing just enough to cover the gap.

The nurse smiled back, unaware she had been spared a moment of grief by a man who understood loss better than anyone in the building.

Later, he forgot the date of a baseball game he had recited to me a hundred times before.

He caught himself mid-sentence.

Paused.

Then said quietly, "That is… incorrect."

He laughed, once. Soft. Like he was humoring himself.

"Long season," I said, trying to match his tone.

He nodded. "Yes. Very long."

The pauses grew longer.

Not empty. Just… searching.

Tommy would stop in the middle of walking, eyes narrowing slightly, as if he were standing at a crossroads only he could see. He never panicked. Never asked for help unless he needed it.

When he did, it sounded like this:

"Elijah," he'd say calmly, "what was I about to do?"

I'd answer.

He'd nod. "Thank you."

And we'd continue.

The staff at Pine Hollows adjusted without making a show of it. That place had learned long ago that dignity mattered more than correction. They offered help the way you offer a coat to someone who's cold, not the way you drag someone inside to warm up.

Tommy appreciated that.

"Predictability," he told me once, voice faintly tired, "is a kindness."

He stopped asking about scores eventually.

That one hurt more than I expected.

Baseball had been the first language he ever trusted. When the questions stopped, I kept telling him anyway. Scores. Players. Dates.

Sometimes he nodded like he recognized them.

Sometimes he smiled like he didn't, but appreciated the effort.

Music stayed longer.

Liszt could still calm him, even when words slipped away. He'd close his eyes and hum, fingers moving against the armrest, pressing keys that only existed for him now.

One afternoon, he frowned suddenly.

"This part," he said. "It should resolve."

179

"It does," I told him gently. "Just takes time."

He relaxed. "Good."

That became a theme.

Trusting me when he could no longer verify.

Trusting the world the way it had never trusted him.

The whistle stayed in the drawer by his bed.

I checked.

Not because I expected him to use it. Because I needed to know it was still there. A promise unbroken. A choice not yet required.

There were bad days.

Days when he woke disoriented, scanning the room like it had betrayed him overnight. Days when language came out sideways, sentences tangling halfway through.

And then there were good days.

Clear ones.

On those days, he'd look at me and say my name without hesitation. He'd ask about my kids. He'd comment on the weather with surprising accuracy.

"You look tired," he told me once, during a stretch when sleep had been hard to come by.

I laughed. "You're one to talk."

He smiled faintly. "Yes. But I have an excuse."

The staff called it progression.

I called it theft.

But Tommy never framed it that way.

"This is expected," he said once, when frustration crept into my voice. "The rate is... acceptable."

"What about you?" I asked. "Ain't you mad?"

He thought about it.

"No," he said finally. "Anger requires certainty."

That sentence stayed with me.

As his world narrowed, so did his focus. He stopped trying to participate in group activities. Too many voices. Too many variables.

He preferred the window in his room, the one that looked out over the small patch of trees behind Pine Hollows.

"I like knowing where the edge is," he explained.

I visited as often as I could.

Sometimes with Maggie. Sometimes alone.

The kids came less as time went on, not because they didn't love him, but because childhood has a way of moving forward even when you beg it to slow down. Tommy never asked where they were.

He knew.

"They're busy," he said once, nodding. "That's correct."

The last conversation we had that felt like us happened on a Tuesday.

Ordinary. Unremarkable.

He was sitting in his chair, blanket over his legs, radio on low.

"Elijah," he said suddenly.

"Yeah?"

"Do you remember the tree?"

My throat tightened. "I do."

He nodded. "Good."

"That was… real," he added, like he was confirming a hypothesis.

"It was," I said firmly. "We carved it ourselves."

He closed his eyes.

"Then I was here," he murmured. "Properly."

I reached out and took his hand.

"You still are."

He squeezed once.

Then relaxed.

After that, the decline accelerated the way it often does once the body realizes the mind has stopped fighting the current. Words became fewer. Recognition intermittent.

But the fear never came.

Not once.

Tommy never screamed. Never begged. Never asked why.

When he forgot my name, he still knew my presence.

"You feel right," he said once, brow furrowed. "I trust that."

The last time I saw him alive, he was sleeping.

Peacefully.

The whistle remained untouched.

He died in the early morning hours, quietly, like someone slipping out of a room after making sure everything was in order.

The nurse tried to call.

Later, she would tell me she tried more than once. That she let it ring longer than policy suggested. That she even left a message she wasn't sure would be heard.

But I didn't answer.

The house was loud that morning. One of the kids was sick. Maggie was exhausted. The phone buzzed somewhere on the counter and disappeared into the noise the way so many small warnings do.

So Tommy died without an announcement.

Quietly. Properly.

That afternoon on the porch, when I finished telling the children about Tommy, about Pine Hollows, about the years that worked, I felt the story settle into my bones like it always did.

The youngest tugged at my sleeve. "Are you done now, Grandpa?"

I shook my head slowly.

"Not yet," I said. "I need you all to go back inside and bundle up. It's still cold out here."

They protested, of course. They always did. But Maggie caught my eye and nodded, already standing.

"Come on," she said gently. "Let Grandpa have a minute."

They went inside, the door closing softly behind them.

I didn't sit.

I went to get my coat, because there are moments in a man's life when remembering isn't enough; when you have to go stand where the truth last existed, just to make sure you didn't imagine it.

Pine Hollows hadn't changed.

The sign was the same. The parking lot lines faded in the same places. The building still held that quiet hum of order and patience, like it had learned long ago that loudness didn't help anyone.

The woman at the front desk recognized me.

Her face shifted, just slightly.

"I'm glad you came," she said softly.

I nodded. "I need to see his room."

She didn't hesitate. "Of course."

The hallway felt longer than it ever had.

When we reached the door, she stopped. "Take your time," she said. "I want you to know... he was peaceful."

I nodded. "That matters."

She left me there.

The room was exactly as Tommy had left it.

The chair by the window. The radio on the table. The blanket folded with care.

Nothing disturbed, nothing dramatic.

Just absence.

I stood and looked, letting the details settle into me the way Tommy would've wanted. Not everything. Just what mattered.

The way the light came through the window.

The silence that didn't feel lonely.

The sense that nothing here had been wasted.

When I left, I closed the door carefully.

32

The house settled into evening the way it always did, with small sounds folding into one another. Dishes clinked. A chair scraped. Someone laughed down the hall. Outside, the woods held their breath the way they do when daylight finally decides to let go.

Elijah found his wife and gave her a hug and kiss, like he did every night before going outside to sit on the porch.

Tonight, he didn't sit at first. He stood at the rail and scanned the edge of the trees, the place where shadow met memory. He let the air fill his lungs and felt both of it at once. The joy. The grief. The long, faithful road that had carried two boys into men and then, finally, into rest.

He thought of radios and baseball and water cold enough to bite. He thought of a mind that counted so the world could be trusted. He thought of a friendship that never asked to be explained.

When he sat, it was with the ease of someone who had stopped keeping score.

Inside the house, Maggie noticed the quiet.

She had learned the difference between ordinary quiet and the kind that arrives with purpose. She looked at the clock. Then at the door. She didn't follow him. Not yet.

Minutes passed.

Then the sound came.

A long, solemn whistle. Not sharp. Not desperate. Full-bodied and sure, like breath released after a lifetime of holding it.

Maggie closed her eyes.

She knew.

The whistle was never meant for Tommy. Not really. It had been given to the one who would finish the race after guiding another safely through it. It was not a call of sorrow. It was a signal of completion.

"Elijah," she whispered, not as a question.

The sound carried through the house, through walls and memory, and then it was gone.

They found him on the porch.

He sat exactly where he had always sat, hands resting easily, the night gathered gently around him. His face held a small smile, the kind that doesn't belong to surprise or relief, but recognition.

Gone.

But not forgotten.

Maggie stood with the children close and did not weep the way people expected. She felt the ache, yes. And the space. But she also felt the deep, unshakable calm of knowing that the work had been done.

Elijah had kept his promises.

And somewhere beyond the reach of time, two friends were together again, and she'd always known that it would end like this. Elijah was in-love with her, but his love of his friend was stronger than any other bond ever made in his lifetime.

Epilogue

The year: 2035

The room at Pine Hollows was filled with light.

New windows. New floors. New paint. The sign on the wall read **Memory & Spectrum Care Wing**, letters clean and hopeful, chosen with intention. Chairs were set in neat rows. Families gathered. Staff stood quietly along the walls, attentive without hovering.

I stepped to the podium and felt my hands steady.

"My name is Daniel Johnson," I said. "I'm the oldest grandson of Elijah Johnson."

I paused, letting the quiet settle the way my grandfather had taught us to do.

"This wing exists because of two men," I continued. "One who measured the world carefully, and one who made sure he was never measured alone."

I told them about a fence that used to divide more than land. About radios turned low and baseball turned loud. About a boy who found safety in numbers and a boy who learned early how to see people clearly.

I told them about Pine Hollows. About dignity. About care that does not rush. About love that makes room.

"And I want you to know," I said, voice steady, "that the story didn't end with loss. It ended with faithfulness."

I looked at the plaque on the wall, newly mounted, the names etched simply, with their favorite bible verse below:

Elijah Johnson & Thomas Miller
Best Friends – Beloved Men

"For God so loved the world, that He sent His only Son, that whoever should believe in Him, should not perish, but have everlasting life." -John 3:16

I finished with the words my grandfather left us, the ones he asked us to remember when the world felt heavy and unclear.

"This is what our grandfather told us when speaking of himself and Tommy, and I have no qualms or reservations in saying that when my grandfather blew that whistle and left this earth, that he was greeted by Jesus and Tommy, and he heard those words: *Well done, my good and faithful servant.*"

The room was quiet again.

But it was a good kind of quiet.

The kind that knows what it's holding.

THE END